D1359664

14 REASONS TO LOVE YOU

A LATOYA NICOLE ANTHOLOGY

DEDICATION

"Everywhere I'm looking now, I'm surrounded by your embrace. Baby I can see your halo, you know you're my saving grace. You're everything I need and more, it's written all over your face. Baby I can feel your halo you know you're my saving grace." Halo- Beyonce

My daughter has been my saving grace without even know it. She has brought me so much joy, and all that matters in this world is her. No one could ever fathom how I feel about her, but I try to explain it every book. So many people have turned their back on her. Treat her like she has the plague, but her uniqueness is what makes her beautiful. You don't have to understand her, just sit back and let her fill your heart with love. My Miracle Monet Riley. An angel walking the earth. My everything. I will forever be grateful, and as long as I have breath in my body, I will give you the world. I love you babes.

ACKNOWLEDGMENTS

Every book I try to acknowledge everyone that has been so much to me. Just know as a whole, I am forever grateful to all of you. If I forget to acknowledge your name, know it's not intentional, and there is always next book. Lol I love my support team so much, just know you are the reason that I am me.

To my bookie boos, it's so much said about this group, but you have given so many people so much help and support, I appreciate the hell out of you. The challenges, spotlights, take overs, promo days all of that helps and just know Latoya Nicole appreciate yall.

Law aka Bestie you are something else. You give me hell, but you keep it real and that's all a friend can ask for. Even though your team beat mine, I still rock

with you. Mama, granny, and even Donovan has started

to grow on me. Marlowe, keep tearing those fields up.

Sky keep running them crazy. Thank you all for letting me

into your world. You're like my family and I love yall.

ZaTasha, I don't know another way I can tell you

thank you, but I will try. We stayed up for hours to come

up with the concept for this book, and I appreciate you

staying on the phone until we had it. You never tell me

no, and you always have my back. I love you girl.

Krissy you just took a spot in my life. Thank you

for being there for me no matter what time it is. I love

you and thank you for helping me make sure my book is

great.

Kb Cole your ass been missing in action, but I

know what it is. I love you and my niece and I appreciate

you being my friend. You are amazing, and I love you. Yall check out her catalog.

A.J Davidson your ass helped me so much with this book, I thank you for being there. I don't know where I would have been without you. I appreciate you cousin for having my back. You're a great person and an amazing author. Yall check out her catalog.

Annitia chile you are just awesome. I love ya girl and keep pushing. I'm glad you chose me to be your AG.

Fay, Monisha, Victoria, Kady, Franny, Kanice I love you squad all day.

To my family Steph, Malik, Johnnae, Shunta, Shenitha, Sheketta, Sheena, Antronna, Jennifer, Ebony Bae... thank yall for supporting me no matter what. I love yall.

To my readers, I promised to put names in each of my books, and these are some more names of people who rock with me. I appreciate you all and I thank you from the bottom of my heart. If you don't see your name, it's okay let me know and I will make sure you're in the next book.

Batina, Lera, Latrice, Courtney, Wyndi, Robin Michelle, Shavozz, Laci, Tamra, Lakimba, Petty aries, Dee Ann, Camille b nurse, Luscioustoy, Tajauna, Simone, Tyhesia, Stacie, Juanita, Denitra, crystal, de'andra, Maria, Nashanda, Shanner, I'Kia, Nefertiti, Quanisha, Janna, Rande, Kristle, sommer, Brittany C., Ebony Phat phat, Sara, Kiesha, Tannesia, Leana, Lashonda, Ms trelle, Davette, Coco Godess, Sierra, Megan, Revondia, Melissa, Sherina, Paula, GiGi, Tamica, Pamela Johnston Ward, Amanda Shmidt, Tiarra,

Danielle, Fatima, Sierra, Marla, Belinda, Karen Rector, Janice, Tecoula, Marsha, Deshana, Wynter, rakiyahmama, Brianna bonner. I love you and I thank you for rocking with me.

MLPP my family my publisher, my pen sisters, my bro, I love yall and keep pushing no matter what. We got this. Yall go check out their work. We coming hard.

All my characters have returned to tell their valentines story giving you 14 reasons to love.

MY GANGSTA

VALENTINE

REASON NUMBER 1

"Something in my soul ain't right, I can't sleep at night. Wondering when the change gone come, feeling like I'm not the only one. Tell me do I turn you off, doctors said it's not my fault. All the neighbors stop and stare, pastor to say to stay in prayer. It will rain, there will be pain. Troubles will come, understand." It will rain- Kelly Price

SUAVE...

Walking around this house, I was going crazy. Everyone know I don't raise my voice, but that's exactly what I feel like doing. A nigga going stir crazy, and Tank ain't getting that shit. She's pregnant again, and I know I should be happy. Instead, it feels like a nigga is sinking.

Maybe if we were still living in Chicago, and I could at least smell the street life I would be okay.

I'm not regretting my decision to walk away from everything, but I'm not sure if this life is cut out for me. I've been down my brother's throat for doing the right thing, but I'm not sure I'm willing to take my own advice.

Every chance I get, I'm on the phone with Smalls asking him what the fuck is going on out there in the streets. Gangsta never fully walked away, and he gets his fix every chance he gets. All the fuck I do is lay in the house and clean up behind my son.

"Suave, can you take Deuce to school today? This baby got me feeling fucked up, and I got the runs." Tank was yelling from the bathroom, and I wanted to tell her ass I hope she shits on herself.

"Yeah, I got it." Walking in the room, I made sure he was dressed and ready to go. Deuce was now three years old, and he was just like me. Didn't do a lot of talking, and said all he needed to say with his actions. His ass was reading a book, and I laughed to myself. This lil nigga stayed in serious mode. Most kids his age wanted to play video games and shit, not his ass. He wanted to mix chemicals together. The nigga had serial bomber written all over him, but if that's what he wanted to do, I was gone be behind his ass lighting the fuse.

"Deuce, you ready to go?" Barely looking up at me, he nodded his head. Walking out the door, we jumped in my whip and headed to his school. His ass ain't even say bye, when we made it to his class. Shaking my head, I walked back to my car and decided to just

drive around. Shit was starting to become

overwhelming, and I didn't like the feeling of being

closed in.

I could go on hits with G, but if I did that, our

wives would know some shit was up. Both of us leaving

together was not a good look, but something was gone

have to shake soon. It wasn't even about the killing, I

just miss the street life. The hanging out and talking shit

with my crew. The fear that came across a nigga face

when they heard my name. If you said Suave out here,

all these niggas thought about was shampoo or body

soap. My ringing phone brought me out of my thoughts.

"What up baby bro?" It seemed like every time I thought about going back, this nigga called me like he could sense it.

"Hey, I got a hit this weekend. I need your help though." Hearing that shit had me interested than a mother fucker.

"What's the details?"

"I know your ass been out the game too long. You got me fucked up if you think I'm saying that shit over the phone. Bring your dumb bitch ass by the house. Paradise is with Tank."

"I'm on the way." I tried to act like I wasn't fazed, but a nigga was damn near doing ninety up a one way trying to get to his house. When I pulled up, I jumped out the car and ran inside his house. Walking around, I was trying to figure out where the nigga was. Stepping in

his bedroom, the smell let me know his ass was in the

bathroom. The nigga had the door open, and started

talking like he wasn't smelling like bird flu.

"You got here quick as hell. Your bitch ass was

standing outside or something?" Not in the mood for

the back and forth, I just wanted to know about the hit.

"Talk." Not needing to say anything else, he knew

when I was serious, and I didn't have to do all the extra

shit to shut shit down.

"So, I got a hit for a million dollars. The only

problem is, it's for two people at the same time. Five

hundred a body. Not thinking, I booked them at the

same time. I would ask Paradise to go with me, but they

both women." I never understood why G fucked the

women he killed, but that was his thing. He told me he does not do that shit no more, but you never know with him.

"This one time, I will help you out. Don't ask me again. What day is it?" Looking at me like he knew I was lying, he smirked and then his face turned serious.

"That's our only problem. It's on Valentine's day." This nigga had to be smoking shit crumbs. There was no way I could pull that over on Tank's ass.

"Nigga have you lost your mind? Or have you forgot who the fuck we are married to?"

"I know, but you also know I can't back out of it. If I don't do the hit, we have to go to war. Which one you think she will be mad at the most? One hit or a full-blown war?" This nigga had a point, but none of this shit was gone blow over well.

"Let me figure something out. I'll get back to you." I don't know how I was gone do this shit, but I knew it wasn't gone be easy.

GANGSTA...

Looking at this nigga face, it took everything in me not to laugh at this nigga. I knew what he was up against, but I know he needed this trip. Just the thought of being back in the streets had my brother looking different.

He thinks he been good at hiding his feelings, but the shit been all up and down those cheap ass sleeves.

Nigga been meaner than pimp getting played out his money. Nobody been wanting to deal with his ass. Tank ignores it, but I was sick of the shit.

I went through the same shit he did, and that's when I got back out there taking hits. His ass just wants to be in the life, I needed to kill. Just the rush of someone's life leaving at the palm of my hand gave a feeling like no other. That nigga was good with leaving it all behind, but I wasn't. Lucifer carried weight, and I was gone make sure mother fuckers feared me even when I was gone.

Wiping my ass, I ran some water to jump in the shower. Shit was feeling good until Paradise snatched the door open bitching.

"What the fuck are these?" Looking at the condoms in her hand, I knew I had to get my ass out of the shower and dry my feet off. A nigga can't be fighting with wet feet. Be sliding all up and through this bitch.

"Paradise, it's not what it looks like. I need them when I do my occasional hits. I'm..." Before I could say anything else, she flicked the box at my ass. Her wrist bout strong as shit, because that box flew at me hard as fuck. When it hit me in the eye, I was no longer trying to explain. The only thing on my mind was getting out this water and beating her ass. Of course, she had other plans.

"Bitch you got me fucked up." Not allowing me out the shower, she knew she had an advantage on my ass. Running towards me fast and hard, she punched me and sent my ass into the Harlem shake. My ass was reaching and grabbing for anything to stop my fall. Not catching nothing but air, the next hit sent me to the floor of the tub. I was pissed, but I couldn't do a damn thing about it.

"You got me fucked up. Dirty dick ass nigga." Plugging her flat irons into the wall, her crazy ass tried to toss them in with my ass. Finally crawling out, I was ready to beat her ass. Knowing she couldn't let me up, her snake ass tried to kick me in the face. Grabbing her foot, I slammed her down to the ground.

Standing up, I was a happy as hell when I landed on my feet. Until she sent my balls flying out my ass. I ain't never been kicked in my dick that hard. Knowing I wasn't gone win this fight today, I had to plead my case.

"Open the box and count the condoms Paradise. I haven't used them. I only take them and make them think we gone fuck." My ass barely got that shit out. "I got the receipt and you can see when I bought the mother fuckers. I haven't used them." When she opened the box to count them, I stood up the best way I could. Catching my breath, I waited until I saw the dumb look on her face.

Knowing I had her ass right where I wanted her, I got a new-found strength. As soon as she opened her mouth to apologize, I gave her an uppercut that sent her ass soaring. She damn near flew to the bed. Walking over to her, I snatched her up and threw her on top of the covers.

Licking the blood off her lips, I stared into her eyes and was happy to know after all these years my baby still loved me. Our fire burned deep, and this was how we loved on each other. No matter what, I wasn't taking no L's. She knew I was going to win at all costs, but I was gone give her some good dick after. Pinning her hands back, I slid my dick to her opening and rammed my shit in. After all these years, her pussy was still tight as African braids, and wet as newborn's mouth.

"You gone take both of these L's baby?" Moaning, she nodded her head. Needing to hear her sexy ass voice, I hit that pussy as hard as I could.

"Yes baby. I'm sorry." Knowing damn well she wasn't sorry, I beat that shit up no matter what she said. That was one of the things I loved most about her. My wife was nowhere near weak. I can't stand a weak ass bitch, and my wife was stronger than damn near all the niggas I knew.

Pulling out, I slid down to her pussy and attacked her shit with my mouth. Sucking that thang like it was my last meal, I ate that shit until her body couldn't take no more.

After two orgasms, I rose up and slid back inside her. Her body was weak as hell, and I was ready to bust. Our baby girl wasn't here, so that mean she had to be with Tank. As bad as she is, I knew they wasn't gone keep her long. Not wanting to miss my nut, I let loose in my wife. Pulling out of her, I laid on my back feeling good as hell. When I felt her mouth wrap around my dick, my shit got brick hard. I may have won the fight,

but she was about to win this round.

TANK...

I don't know how I let Paradise trick me into

keeping Kenya, but I was ready to drop kick her ass back

to their house. This little girl was beyond bad. I never

seen anything like it. How in the fuck someone has a

baby this bad is beyond me. She was two years old, and I

swear she was a monster. I was already pissed that I was

cleaning up some experiment Deuce had been working

on, the fluids were everywhere when I came across a

spot that smelled like piss.

Is this lil nigga using piss for his experiment? Not thinking anything of it, I continued to clean. When I got in the hallway, it was a pile of shit at the door and I slid straight in it.

"Suave, what the fuck is this?" Walking in the hallway, he looked down and laughed.

"Your niece left you a present it seems. Clean that shit off your foot. I don't want your ass trailing the shit through my house." The nigga didn't even offer to help, he walked his ass back in the room without another word. This nigga been walking around the house, acting like he was ready to get a divorce. This nigga was not happy and thought no one noticed. I was sick of all this shit.

Hopping in the bathroom, I stuck my foot in the tub and cleaned it off. After cleaning everything up, I walked towards the front and slipped again. Looking down, it was another pile of shit. When I looked over at Kenya ass, she was by the tv squatting taking another shit. Her ass was doing this shit on purpose and she had me fucked up.

"I'm about to beat your lil ass. Get the fuck over here. Nasty ass lil girl. Who raised your ass?" Knowing she was too young to understand half the shit I said, I was even more pissed. A bitch had tears in her eyes as I turned to go wash this shit off again. Suave was standing his ass in the hallway laughing so hard he was bent over. If I wasn't scared he would kill my ass, I would toss some at his ass. This would be the shit he found funny. Nigga ain't laughed in months now he all bent over slapping

his ashy ass knee. When I walked towards him, I gave

him the shittiest look I could muster up.

"Get your niece, and both of yall get the fuck out

of my house. Nasty ass bastards." Walking in the

bathroom, I slammed the door and cried. Hearing him

chuckle only made it worse. I don't know if I was pissed

for real, or if the baby was causing my hormones to rise.

Either way, I was over this shit.

After an hour of being in there, I finally came out

and went to our room. Suave was sitting there in the

dark, and I didn't like the look on his face. Lately, it

seems like I was the only one trying to make our

marriage work. Knowing my husband better than he

knew his self, I made special plans for Valentine's Day. It

was my last hope at trying to fix our marriage and I prayed it worked. It seemed like we were on our last leg, but we been through too much for me to lose him now.

"Would you be mad if we celebrated Valentine's Day before or after? We just need to do it on another day, instead of that one." Making sure he saw the look on my face, I stared at him for a few minutes.

"Are you serious? Who the fuck is she? You and that bitch got me fucked up if you think that shit flying. That is a couple's holiday, and you think you gone spend that shit away from me?" Shaking his head, I could tell I got under his skin. His veins popped, but he didn't raise his voice.

"I'm not gone tell you again to watch how you talk to me. Fix your fucking face, and your attitude or the conversation is done." Waiting on me to calm down, he looked at me until my face was how he wanted it.

"It's a fucking day that was made up. You know how I feel about you, and it shouldn't take one day out of the year for you to know what you mean to me. It ain't no other bitch, and it's business." Smirking, I stood directly in front of him.

"What business you got Suave? We don't do shit but take care of our son. I know we aren't in need of money, so what is it? If it's not a bitch, tell me what it is." His entire face changed, but he still didn't get loud.

"None of your fucking business." Getting up, he left out the room leaving me defeated. This nigga talked to me like he resented me. I know he miss his old life, but he chose to walk away. It was his decision alone.

When I got out of my coma, all of the plans were made, and he put my ass on a plane. I had no idea we were living here, until our honeymoon. Which is why I'm so lost on how the fuck he is blaming me for this shit.

All I wanted was for us to go back to the way we were. I love my husband, but I was losing him. My ass was still going forward with my plans for Valentine's Day. I had to fix our marriage, and this was the only way I knew how.

Laying under the covers, I cried thinking of where we are now. Not wanting to put all this stress on the baby inside my stomach, but I couldn't help it. I laid in the same spot crying for two hours. When I felt him climb back in the bed with me, my tears dried, and I was finally able to fall asleep.

PARADISE...

My legs were too weak, and Tank or Suave was

banging on my door. I already knew it was them because

they were babysitting Kenya. This damn girl couldn't be

kept by nobody. Crawling to the door, I opened it and

Suave looked at me laughing. This nigga was practically

dragging Kenya and her bag.

"Nigga don't be pulling my baby like that I'll shoot

your ass in your left ball. You had a boy so your right one

is kind of empty." This nigga looked at me like I was

crazy.

"What? You know what, never mind. Get this lil

girl. She done shitted all over my damn house. Tank over

there mad as hell."

"First of all, it is a proven fact one of your balls is smaller when you have a baby. The Sex determines which one. Second of all, babies shit. How the fuck yall mad at her for doing something that all babies do? Yall be on that bullshit. Give me my damn baby." Snatching her from his petty ass, I attempted to walk away bowlegged as hell. Thinking about Valentine's Day, I stopped in my tracks.

"Oh, by the way, if you think that you and your sleepy neck ass brother gone treat us like some side bitches, you got us fucked up. What kind of husband leaves their wives on the most special day of the year. Yall bitches got some nerve, but you can try me if you want to." This nigga laughed at me.

"You can try that tough shit with your man, but I'm not him. I'm not gone hold back on your ass, I'm gone beat you like you a fucking nigga. Your ass like to play crazy, mother fucker ain't no word for me. Now take your dumb ass on, talking about some damn one nut bigger. My balls big bitch and they the same damn size." Smacking him on his arm, we laughed, and I walked off on his mean ass. That nigga was worse than G, I don't care what nobody says. That nigga was that silent storm.

"Your ugly ass brother just brought the baby back. It's a damn shame how they treat our baby. She bad, but she ain't that damn bad." Getting his sexy ass off the bed, his dick was standing at attention.

"Your ass in denial, I damn near left her on the neighbor's porch a few times. Keep an eye on her while I go take a shower. If she gets in my shit, I'm gone beat both of yall ass." Standing in my kicking position, I let that nigga know he don't want these problems.

Once he was done in the shower, I went and got my ass in. I had to go meet up with Tank, so we could go over our plans for Valentine's Day. The men had no idea what we were up to, and I was excited as hell. This was the most excitement we had around here in years. Kenya was the only one that seems to keep everybody on their toes.

Damn shame when your baby is the only reason any of our ass is getting a kick out of life. This shit was for the birds, and for once I agree with Suave. Gangsta was another one that was living it up. Whenever he got

bored, he would go and do a hit. No matter what I say,

he leaves my ass here and make me stay with the

demon child.

Getting out the shower, I wondered how in the

fuck this became my life. To think, I'm the one that

begged for this shit. G told me over and over, the life we

lived wasn't for a child. My ass fucked up and damn near

had him killed trying to prove a point. Now my ass sitting

here looking stupid, and bored. Don't get me wrong, I

don't regret Kenya, but my life has done a three sixty.

My ass is bored, and I can't wait until Valentine's day.

We about to shake the fucking table.

Climbing out of the shower, I dried off and put my

clothes on. G ass was knocked out, but he was just

talking shit about me keeping an eye on her. Throwing a

right hook at his ass, he didn't even stir in his sleep.

Sliding my shoes on, I felt some gushy shit. Taking my

foot out, I looked down and I wanted to throw up. This

bad ass mother fucker shitted in my damn shoe.

Starting the process all over again, I got the fuck

out of there and left her with G. I hope she shits in his

damn mouth. Even though I loved my pink Maserati, the

shit just didn't look right driving it out here. Especially

living this boring ass life. They ass lived right down the

street, but I needed to be out of the house, so we were

meeting up at the mall.

A bitch needed some type of therapy, and retail

was the best one. We agreed to meet in the Chanel

store, and as soon as I walked in, I knew this was the

right decision. I saw a suit that was to die for, and I couldn't wait to wear that shit on Valentine's Day. When I looked over to my right, Tank's ass was already here trying on shoes.

"Girl why your ass ain't tell me you were here? My ass thinking you were late and I started shopping."

"I been here about thirty minutes. It's almost like me and Suave can't even be in the same room. That nigga is mean as hell, and I just don't know what to do anymore. This baby is wearing my ass out, and I'm just tired Paradise.

My ass didn't go through this with Deuce. Feet swollen, my nose done spread, and my hip hurts all damn day. That's probably why my husband doesn't want me anymore." When her ass started crying, I was ready to get the fuck up out of there. Everybody knows I

don't do feelings.

Patting her on her head, I tried to comfort her in

some kind of way. I had no idea what to do for her.

When me and G were on the outs, I just pulled my gun

on his ass and left. We fought, and I didn't take no shit

off him. I was that nigga I'll beat your ass type of bitch,

and G knew it. Not that he backed down, that nigga

would fight my ass like I was one of the homies.

"Bitch if you gone pat my head like I'm a poodle at

the pound, we can just change the subject." Laughing, I

hugged her and went to try on a pair of heels that a

bitch had to have.

"Excuse me ma'am, you can't try those on. We don't have cleaner in here." What the fuck this bitch ass shoe rep say to me?

"Bitch the fuck you say?"

"You umm have feces on your foot. We can't allow you to try our shoes on." Looking down, I didn't get all of Kenya shit off me. Aggravated ass fuck, this bitch needed to know not to fuck with me. Rubbing the shit off my foot, I stood up and wiped it across her lip.

"Now bring me these in red, size eight." That hoe ran off in tears. I hate weak women.

"Bitch, your ass gone go to jail. I'm gone, Suave would fuck around and leave my ass in there the way he feels about my ass. Nigga leave me and the baby on the green mile."

"I wish the fuck she would. She better have my damn heels when she walks her ass out that door." Clutching my gun just in case I needed to shoot my way out of here, I was happy the bitch was smart enough to just bring me my damn shoes. Yes, I definitely couldn't wait until Valentine's Day.

REASON NUMBER 2

"Our relationship is suffering, try to give you what I never had. You say I don't know how to love baby, and I say show me the way. I keep my feelings deep inside, I, shadow them with my pride. I'm trying desperately, baby just work me with me. Teach me how to love, show me the way to surrender my heart." Teach Me- Musiq

TANK...

"Why the fuck won't you look at me Kendyl? You're acting as if I did something to you, and all I am trying to do is figure out how to fix us." Suave wouldn't even talk to me, and we weren't even into it. I have no idea what was going on with him. It seems like we were good until we watched a movie last night. I love Paid in

Full, but if it was gone cause this type of division in my

home, then I was throwing this shit the fuck away.

"Tank, if you yell at me one more time, we are

going to have a problem for real. Sometimes a nigga

don't feel like talking, and lately, with the shit that you

been pulling you making the shit easy. Now go the fuck

to bed before you piss me off."

"How many times do I have to tell your ass that

you are not my daddy. We are married, and lately you

been treating my ass like you don't want to be here. If

you don't want to be here, then get the fuck out."

Before I could say anything else, he snatched my ass up.

He pushed me so hard, we went through the balcony

doors.

If the nigga didn't love me just a little, my ass would be dead. My big ass almost tipped over the fucking balcony, until he caught me.

"Lashay, you are pushing me to a limit I'm not trying to go. I don't know why the fuck you want to keep testing me, but you better get your shit together. I'm going through something, and you just need to let me get through it." He said that hit like it's that simple, and it's not. I refused to let him stay in this slumber. If I did, it could be the end of us. He keeps saying it's not me, but it feels like he no longer wants me.

"This baby got me ugly, and fat. You don't want me no more and I get that, but I'll fix it when the baby gets here. I'm sorry that I'm not attractive baby, but I can't help it." Not being able to help it, the tears came falling down making me look even worse. Grabbing me to him, he softened up.

"Tank, nothing you do will ever make me stop being attracted to you. You are beautiful to me, and you always will be. Listen, a nigga old. Maybe I'm going through a midlife crisis or some shit. Either way, it has nothing to do with you. Just give a nigga the space he is asking for to get his shit together."

"If that's true, then why are you trying to spend Valentine's Day without me? Who is she?" You could tell he was pissed, his damn vein almost knocked my ass out.

"I'm not fucking with another bitch Tank. Look at you." Turning my head away from him, I felt ugly as hell. "Look at me." When I didn't, he got pissed. "LOOK AT

ME." It was odd hearing him raise his voice, the nigga shook me to my core. When I raised my face, the stare he gave me had my pussy wet. When our lips touched, I was out of my pants before he could change his mind about fucking a whale.

Wrapping my leg around his waist, he slid his fingers up and down my slit. All we have done was argue the past few weeks, and sex was the last thing on our minds.

"My pussy wet as hell. Put it in my mouth Tank." I guess my big ass was moving too slow. "I'll put it in my mouth. I want to taste you." Right there on the concrete, he got down on his knees. Looking around, I tried to see if anybody was able to see us up here. That shit didn't last long. Once he started sucking on my clit, I had to close my eyes and hold on for the ride. After I came all on that tongue, he lifted me up, and laid me on the table.

"Open that pussy up." Spreading my legs, I prayed this table held my big ass. Pushing my legs back, he watched as he slid inside. You could hear the wetness, and I was ready to cum just from contact.

"You the only mother fucker I want. Don't ever forget that shit. Now who pussy is this?" Not being able to answer, I was trying to focus on taking the dick and not falling. When he slammed his big ass dick in me to get my attention, the shit worked. "Who pussy is this?"

"Yours baby. Now get out my cervix before your ass bring this baby down early." Grabbing me roughly by my hair, he bit my lip. His strokes slowed down, but it was intense. Grabbing my breasts, he used them as

leverage as his strokes increased.

"Fuck girl. You got this dick cumin'." Our bodies

started to shake at the same time, and for once in a long

time, it felt like we were in sync. Laying on my chest, he

tried to catch his breath. My prayers must have fallen on

deaf ears, because that table gave out on our ass.

Between shit all over my house, and this weak ass table,

I was having a rough ass day. He better be lucky the sex

was bomb, or I would be ready to kick his ass.

Laughing at my face, he helped me off the ground

and carried me inside. It felt like I had my man back. Shit

was starting to look up.

****

Looking around the room, I see Suave ass was up already. Since I'm in a good mood, I decided to go cook my man some breakfast. My ass went in there and whipped up a meal. Assuming he was in his man cave, I made him a plate. A bitch had made grits, eggs, sausages, bacon, pancakes, and I had a bowl of fruit. When a nigga put it down in the bedroom, he will have a bitch singing amazing grace while cooking all the groceries in the fridge.

"Baby, I hope you're hungry. Your wife threw down for you." Walking in his man cave, I gave him his food. This nigga grabbed it and sat it down. Not bothering to even look up at me. I don't know why I thought we were in a better place after last night, but I was wrong as fuck. This nigga was still treating me like

the damn ugly step sister.

"Did you already eat?" Never turning his face

towards me, he acted as if I was getting on his nerves.

"No Tank I haven't. I'm just not hungry. I'm

counting my money and checking numbers if you don't

mind giving me a minute." Walking out of the room, I

slammed the door. Sitting down on the bed, I heard our

alarm go off and knew he was leaving. This nigga had me

fucked up. Still having a tracker on his phone, I watched

to see where his ass was going. Twenty minutes later, I

had his location and I was on the way.

Making sure I grabbed my Beretta, I got out of the

car. I had no idea who was in this house, but if the shit

wasn't looking good, they ass was about to catch a fade.

I might be losing my husband, but that hoe was going to

lose her thoughts. Creeping up to the door the best way

I could, I tried not to make any noise. Grabbing the knob,

I headed in grateful it was open. Walking around the

entire first and second floor, I couldn't find Suave. His

car was outside, so I knew he was here.

About to leave, I saw a door to the kitchen with a

lock hanging from it. My nerves kicked in because

everybody know them locked doors mean crazy. Easing

down the stairs, the hairs were standing up on my arms

and I got the same feeling I did when Gangsta would

come in the room.

Reaching the bottom of the stairs, I almost shit

myself. Suave was just sitting there with a shot gun in his

hand. He was just staring at the nigga he had tied and

hanging from the ceiling. It was creeping me the fuck

out, and I was scared to say anything. It's like his ass was

in a zone. Finally getting up the nerve, I decided to

interrupt his serial moment.

"Baby what are you doing?" I'm not sure if he

heard me, because he didn't even blink. "Suave, did you

hear me." When I yelled, he finally responded.

"What are you doing here? We not about to go

through this shit again. YOU ARE NOT A NIGGA. TAKE

YOUR ASS THE FUCK HOME, AND DON'T MAKE ME TELL

YOU AGAIN." This nigga never raises his voice, and I

must admit, I was scared. Not scared enough to check

his ass though.

"I asked you a fucking question? You got about

ten seconds to tell me what the fuck is going on." Taking

the safety off my gun, this nigga was about to get his ass

lit up. I was ready for a fight, but this nigga sighed and

the look he gave me broke my heart.

"I'm not happy. I dead ass don't wanna be here.

Every day, it feels like I'm drowning. This is not how my

life is supposed to be going. I was King of the fucking Chi.

Now I'm, daddy fucking daycare." Not sure what to say, I

stood there silent. My husband just told me he was no

longer happy with me. Holding his shot gun up, he

pointed it at the guy. Lowering it, he walked away. You

could see how he was struggling with his self not to kill

him.

"Bring your ass the fuck on, and if you even think

about saying some smart shit, think about your life. I'm

not in the mood, and the way I feel right now I will kill

you. Let's go."

This nigga had me fucked up, and it was only one

thing I could do. I shut my ass up and took my ass home.

I was crazy, but not that damn crazy. Now was not the

time to be trying to take a stand.

I would have my words with Suave, but this

moment was not it. Besides, I needed to process what

the fuck he just said to me. This shit just broke my heart,

and with each step I fought back tears. All I needed to do

was keep us afloat until Valentine's Day.

GANGSTA...

"You told her what nigga? Are you fucking crazy? That girl is the best thing that happened to you and your dumb ass treating her like she the first piece of bread. Yet, everybody always thought you was the smart brother." I couldn't believe the shit Suave was doing. His ass around here acting like Tank don't make him happy enough. I had to admit, when I first met her, I didn't like her ass.

She was mad annoying at first, always popping the fuck up on some rah-rah shit. Now, she was my sister. When we thought we lost him, all we had was each other.

"Nigga you the same mother fucker that treated Paradise like Freezer burn. Don't come at me."

"That shit was different bro. The bitch faked a kidnapping and tried to kill me. Not to mention she slept with Sin nasty ass." Suave knew damn well it wasn't the same thing.

"Fuck both of you niggas. Yall gone stand here and act like I ain't here. I hope she put your ass out." We laughed at Paradise because I honestly forgot she was in the room. "Why you just won't tell her what the problem is? Why make her feel like it's her? I'm not into all this secret shit. If I was her I would just beat your ass and move the fuck on."

"Shut up. Damn. Bro, even though she talks too much, I agree with my baby. Just tell her. Nigga you want to kill somebody, you act like you cheating and shit."

"Yall don't understand, Tank is not like Paradise. She does what she has to when needed, but she is not a killer. Yall will do that shit together, but Tank can't even be in the same room with me when I do that shit. She will never want to move back to Chicago. We almost lost too much and asking her something like that will end us." I understood what he was saying, Paradise was one of a kind. That's why I would never let her ass go, but my brother wasn't giving Tank enough credit.

"Look, all I'm saying is you never know. You are taking her decision from her, and that shit ain't cool. You say telling her will end yall, but the shit you are doing now definitely will. Get your shit together before you lose her. Valentine's day is close, and you don't need to be going through this shit when that day come. I'm with you no matter what you decide."

"I hear you, but I got this. Me and Tank are different. Do your shit your way, and let me do my shit my way."

"Whatever nigga. Since yall into it, can you take Kenya home with yall. I need some pussy and her ass do too much."

"You got me fucked up. That baby shitted all over my fucking house. Keep her lil nasty ass right here. It don't even be lil shit neither. Her funky ass sits right there and squat out some grown man shit." Paradise didn't laugh because Kenya shitted in her shoes, but I found the shit funny as hell. She didn't fuck with me, I guess her lil ass knew better.

"Aight bro. Now get the fuck out. Go talk to your girl, and try to work yall shit out. All I know is your ass better be ready, and with a clear head."

"Yeah, I'm out. I hope she scrape your shit up with her teeth."

"Your bitter ass acting like you can't get no pussy. You got a wife, go sex her ass down." His ass started looking all mad again. I'm playing counselor when all I did was want to play in some pussy.

"If I fuck her, she thinks shit be good. I'm just not in the mood for all that shit. I need a clear head, and we just not in that space right now."

"Nigga, did you not hear me say I was trying to hit my wife. Get your whining ass out. In here sounding like a damn bitch. You don't want our advice, and you said you got it. Guess you gone handle your own nut tonight too. Well I'm not, I got some pussy. When you leave, I can stick my dick in it." You could tell this nigga wanted to hit my ass, but he knew better.

"Fuck you Gangsta. I'll see you tomorrow." As soon as he walked out, I damn near drug Paradise to the room.

"Baby wait, I have to go put Kenya to bed. You know that baby bad as hell. She would be into all kind of shit. Give me ten minutes. I'm gone give her some Benadryl, it shouldn't take long." I swear this girl was crazy as hell.

"You better not drug my baby." The fact that she didn't laugh had me a lil worried. Kenya ass was so damn bad, the shit might not work no way. Jumping in the shower while she was in there with the baby, I washed

my ass to get these balls smelling right for her ass.

Making sure my hygiene was straight, I figured I

may as well lay naked since she was about to get this

dick. Climbing in the bed, I had to stop myself from

throwing up. Jumping up and moving the cover back, I

was about to go fuck Kenya up. Her nasty ass shitted in

my damn bed.

PARADISE...

These niggas are getting on my nerves, and I was

over all the bullshit. My ass was ready to tell everybody

what the fuck was going on. Too many damn secrets

weren't healthy, and I wanted no parts of this shit. I

couldn't wait until Valentine's Day, everything should go back to normal.

They know I don't do well with feelings, and I ain't about to start now. The moment Gangsta told me we were moving out here with his brother and Tank, I knew it was gone turn into some mushy shit. It was starting to rub off on me, and I needed to take my ass on a hit with G. The shooting range or something. That's where the fuck I should have been, instead my ass was on the way to meet Tank. Again.

Between her and Suave, I was losing my fucking mind. I'm so glad me and G are in a different space now, but knowing what we went through at one point, I knew I had to. It was a time that Gangsta wasn't trying to hear what I had to say, and it forced me to do something stupid. That was the only reason I was pulling up to this damn boutique.

Walking inside, I damn near wanted to go back home. Who the fuck looks at clothes while they are crying and shit? Fuck, I'm not good with this shit.

"Tank if your ass don't stop all that crying shit, I'm gone beat your ass."

"Don't act like you forgot what these hands do. Don't make me beat box your taco eating ass. Bitch I'm always crying because I'm pregnant. Get over it."

"You tried it. Bitch you snaked me, and I still gave your ass hell. Now if you fought for your marriage as hard as you tried to fight me, I wouldn't be playing counselor every other damn day. You already know what his problem is, and you have a plan. WHAT THE

FUCK ARE YOU CRYING FOR? Let's just stick to what we said and keep it the fuck moving." Damn, how hard could this shit be. My ass was sick of this shit. She act like she don't already know what the fuck it is.

"Whatever, you can go the fuck back home. I wasn't even crying over Suave ass." Now I was confused.

"What the fuck were you crying for then?" She looked at me like she was ashamed.

"Because they were out of steaks at the diner across the street. I've been craving that shit all damn day. Pissed me the fuck off." I was two seconds away from slapping this bitch to the dirt.

"You have got to be shitting me, right?"

"No, but your daughter is shitting. Probably all over your house right now. So, imma let you get to it.

Everything is a go for tomorrow, and I already have our tickets. My people in Chicago already got shit set up, and all we have to do is show up. Meeting over, now get the fuck out of my damn face before I lick your elbow. Ass over there looking like butter pecan ice cream." Now I know this mother fucker was tripping.

"Bitch I know you were gay for the stay, but I ain't with that shit. You pushing me to beat that ass. Stupid ass in here crying over some damn steak." I damn near slapped her ass before I walked out of the store. She had shit fucked up. I wonder if I was this crazy when I was pregnant.

Heading home, I laughed as I pulled into this spot to grab me a steak before I head in. As soon as they were done, and passed me my food. I took a picture and

sent it to that hoe. Laughing, I headed home.

Walking in the door, the smell of shit hit my nose.

I'm about to give this little girl up for adoption. How the

hell did she get so trifling?

"G, where are you?" When he didn't answer, I

walked in the room and he was in there about to square

up with Kenya. Laughing, I grabbed my baby and took

her to the bathroom to bathe her. Why my baby

couldn't be more like Deuce? He was so sweet, and mild

mannered. After we were done, I read to her and put

her to sleep. I only had her for an hour and I was wore

out. I would never tell Tank, but I damn sure agreed with

Suave's ass on this shit.

Nobody life deserved to be this boring. Even though I was the one that begged for this shit, this is not the life for a person that killed so many damn people. My ass needed to smell blood sometimes, and not the shit that leaks out of my cat. This plan that tank had up her sleeve was going to benefit all of us. My ass couldn't wait until tomorrow. I'm over all this bullshit.

SUAVE...

"Deuce, what the hell is this shit all over my house? It better not be some shit that's gone explode on my damn floor. Save that shit for school." It was early in the morning, and Tank's ass was already yelling.

"Don't talk to my fucking son like that. If you got an issue, handle that shit within your damn self. Come here son." He walked over to me, and you could tell she hurt his feelings. That damn baby was making her mean as shit. It had to be a girl, because her ass didn't act like that when she was pregnant with Deuce.

"What you been working on son? Show me what all of this is."

"I'm trying to work on chemical change. I can't get it to combine into one." Not knowing what the hell he was talking about, I just nodded my head. He talked his ass off, and I felt dumb as hell.

"That's good son. I'm glad you have something you like. When daddy comes back from his trip, we can work on it together. Imma need something to do so my ass don't be bored out of my mind. So, what you say?

You gone teach me?"

"Daddy I can't wait until you come back. We have

to get new stuff. I love you so much." Laughing at his

excitement, we walked out of the door, so he could go

to school. He was different, but I loved the shit out of

my son. Nigga was gone be more than me one day, and I

was going to make sure he was gone have all the

support he needed.

Dropping him off at school, I headed back to my

boring ass house to pack. I knew Tank was going to be

mad as hell, so I tried to do the shit as fast as I could. As

soon as I walked in the door, she was standing there

staring at me all weird like.

"Fuck you standing there looking like Michael Myers for and shit?" A nigga was ready to take off running with the look she was giving me. When she didn't answer, I headed to the room and I could hear her behind me. Looking back, her ass was doing the serial killer walk. I loved my wife, but I was gone lay her ass out if she thought she was gone come at me with a knife. Moving as quick as I could, I threw my stuff in my bag occasionally looking over my shoulder. This mother fucker stood there looking the entire time.

"Baby, I will be back tomorrow morning. I have something special planned for you, and I'm sorry for making you feel like it was you. Everything will be good after tonight. I promise." When I tell you, her ass didn't blink. Her ass didn't blink. She had my ass shook.

Tank ass didn't say a word, just followed me everywhere I moved. Damn near running out the door, I jumped in my whip and headed to G house. The look she was giving me, almost made me want to turn around and go back. She has never looked at me like that, and she had me feeling a way. For the first time since we been together, I think my wife has given up on me. When I get back, I will make it up to her. This trip, I needed this trip. Even if I didn't want to go, I would have because G needed me. His ass could be killed if he didn't complete the hit. Pulling up to their house, I had so much shit on my mind. When I walked in the door, he was waiting on me and ready.

"Let's roll bro. Once we get there, we got some shit to do and handle first." Kissing Paradise goodbye, we headed to the airport to board our private plane.

That was the best investment we could have ever made.

The flight was long, and my ass slept the entire

way. As soon as my feet hit the pavement, I felt new

again. This was the way a nigga was supposed to feel.

Everything smelled different, my blood was pumping

different, and I was in a better fucking mood already.

"Your cry baby ass happy now?" Not in the mood

for G shit, I looked around for Smalls. This nigga was

never on time.

"Bitch fuck you. I remember your ass telling me

the same fucking thing. You forgot your ass was around

here sneaking around killing people. Fuck out of my

face." Before G could response, I spotted Smalls and

headed his way.

"My nigga. Your ass look old. Fuck is wrong with you? Is it curable?" Him and G laughed, and I walked off. They were determined to piss me the fuck off.

"Suave wait up. Calm your sissy ass down. You the only sensitive ass gangsta I know. Nigga you stay in your fucking feelings." Smalls didn't realize how close he was to getting his ass knocked out.

"Fuck yall." Jumping in his car, we ended up at his house. "You niggas trying to get me killed. You know Nik bald headed ass gone tell my girl I was here."

"Paradise said the last time they were there, she was showing them pictures and she had hair. Fuck happened?" I couldn't do shit but laugh at G.

"Man, what pic yall looked at? She ain't never had no hair with me. Since the day I met her, the mother fucker had pregnancy test drop of a piss length of hair."

Me and G looked at each other lost as hell.

"Nigga fuck are you talking about?"

"You know when they take a pregnancy test, you

only need a drop of piss. That's how long her hair is

nigga. Like I said, she ain't never had no hair with me."

Getting out of the car, we got our laughs out before we

headed in. As soon as we walked in, Nik took off

running. Her hair was matted down to her head, and you

could tell she wasn't expecting company.

"Yall ugly asses better not laugh either." Smalls

was trying not to laugh, and it wasn't making it easier on

us.

"She about to beat your ass." G was a shit starter,

but I was thinking the same thing.

"Nigga you know damn well my bitch can't fight. Yall niggas shut the fuck up while I go eat some pussy to calm her bald-headed ass down." Grabbing a piece of chicken, he headed in their room. My ass thought we were about to get into some shit, now they ass was about to have me in more trouble than I was. Tank was about to fuck my ass up.

****

"Wake yall dumb ass up, and let's go. It's time." Smalls was standing over us. We had falling asleep, and our ass spent the entire day here sleep.

"Hey yall." Nik was standing there with a twisted ass wig on.

"What's up." We went to head out the door, and I turned back to Nik. "Stay out of my business or I will shift that wig in place." Smalls and Gangsta laughed as she tried to fix her wig. Walking out the door, we jumped back in Smalls car. He was dropping G off first, and then going with me to my hit.

"Yall gone stop talking about my bitch. She just need some Dr. Miracles. They ran out of the kind for course hair." Not wanting to stir the pot any further, we laughed under our breath. Zoning out, everyone in the car got quiet. We all needed to be ready because niggas in Chicago didn't play. We had a different way about us in my city.

Pulling up to G's drop off, you can tell he was in go mode when he grabbed his bag. Knowing my brother was the best at what he did, I wasn't worried about him.

That nigga was a beast, and I was proud of the name he made for his self.

On the way to our spot, I started to think if I made a mistake. Not because I didn't want to do this, but I'm not sure if it was worth me losing Tank. She was my rock, and I been treating her like shit because I was going through something. Knowing now was not the time to call her, I would make sure I did when the job was over. We would spend the rest of Valentine's Day on the phone together.

Once I did this hit, I was just gone have to get over the shit. Yea a nigga wanted to come back home, but I loved my family more. It wasn't even her idea that we go to Hawaii, it was mine. My ass been punishing her over a decision that I made. I hadn't even realized the car had

stopped.

"Nigga you good? Listen, whatever is on your

mind, you need to clear your head before you go in

there. Shit can get real, and I need you to be good." You

could tell he was concerned, and that's why he was my

nigga for life.

"I've been treating Tank bad. My ass been missing

this shit, and I don't know how to deal with the shit. I've

barely said two words to her in months. The only person

I deal with is Deuce. Shit is all bad back at home, and

that's on me. Today is Valentine's Day, and my ass is

here because I'm not ready to let go of the streets." He

just looked at me for a while before he spoke.

"I've watched that girl save your life more than once. Nigga, she searched the entire city looking for your ass when everybody thought your ass was dead. I still can't believe they ass had a ghost in my house." Looking at his ass like he lost his mind, he laughed and got back on track.

"What I'm trying to say is this, that girl loves you. Nigga we done had our backs against the wall, and she came in guns blazing saving our ass. Just know this, she ain't going nowhere. Now get your soft ass out the car. I don't do that gay shit, but they may have room for you down at the booty house."

What he said was the truth, and my baby wouldn't leave me over this. She didn't even leave me when she thought I was dead. I got this, I just had to get over this shit I was in. My ass was gone have to allow Tank to help me through it.

"Aight nigga come on. I'm ready. Let's go tuck these niggas in." Getting out of the car, I grabbed my bag. Gun in hand, we headed into the house. The shit was eerily quiet, and something was off. Before I could say something to Smalls, he pushed me forward.

Walking through, this house was big as hell and I was tired of playing find the niggas. Rounding the corner, it was rose petals all over the floor. They ass had their bitches over here for Valentine's Day, and now we were gone have to kill they ass too.

Following the petals, they were leading to the basement. This nigga was weird as fuck taking his bitch to the basement to spend the most special day of the year. That had me thinking about Tank again, and I had to shake that shit off.

When we got all the way in, the rose petals led to a table. On this table, two niggas were strapped down asshole naked. What the fuck kind of kinky shit they were on, and where the fuck were the women? These niggas had ball gags in their mouths, and they looked scared. The bitches must have robbed they ass. Looking over at Smalls, he didn't look shocked like me. His ass actually looked amused.

"What the fuck." When I got to the table, I didn't give a fuck what was going on. I was here to do a job, and I was going to do it.

"Happy Valentine's Day baby." Hearing her voice, I was ready to beat her ass. Tank ass was always following a nigga on bullshit, and this time she went too far.

Turning towards her, I had fire in my eyes. Before I could

beat her ass, G and Paradise came into view. What the

fuck was going on.

"Okay, I give up. What is this shit. A nigga lost."

Everybody was smiling and shit, and I was ready to go

the fuck off.

"Well baby, everybody knows how you been

walking around acting like you done lost your best friend

and shit. Even though you thought I didn't, I knew what

was going on. So, my gift to you is this. Everybody

helped me get you here for the most special Valentine's

Day, ever." Shocked was an understatement.

"You did all of this for me? That's why I love you

baby. Let me go and kill this nigga, so we can go the fuck

home. Your pussy is about to be WOE." Everybody

laughed, but they still had this weird look on their face.

"What?"

"Baby, we are home. Happy Valentine's Day."

Picking her up around my waist, I was about to slide her

this dick right now.

"No the fuck yall nasty asses ain't. It's two naked

ass niggas on the table, and yall trying to fuck." Kissing

her one last time, I laughed at Smalls ass.

"Tank give me a minute to handle them. Go

upstairs and sit with your mouth open so you can get

ready to suck this dick. I'm hornier than a mother

fucker." Grabbing a scalpel out of my bag, I walked over

to the table.

"Do you know what this is? Just nod if you do."

When the niggas nodded, I looked over to G. "Do you know who he is?" They nodded again. "Good, then you know what the fuck is about to happen to you. G you get upper, and I get lower. No face, no case."

"I swear something is wrong with you niggas. Sick ass bastards. It's good to have yall home."

ADDICTED TO MY

VALENTINE

REASON NUMBER 3

"It could all be so simple, but you'd rather make this hard. Loving you is like a battle, and we both end up with scars. Tell me who I have to be, to gain some reciprocity. No one loves you more than me, and no one ever will." Ex Factor- Lauryn Hill

AURI...

Flying through traffic, I was trying to make it to my destination. I needed to do what I had to, and still beat Deleon home. His ass says he trust me, but the nigga sure don't act like it. I had to check in with him just to go wipe my ass. The shit was driving me crazy, and I had no idea what to do.

A couple of years ago, I was this scared naïve girl who didn't know which way was up. At my graduation, Deleon proposed to me, but we have yet to get married. I think the nigga was scared I was going to be back in the crack house.

The way shit been going lately, sometimes I felt like going back. Those times were less stressful. Even though I was fucked up, my ass didn't have a care in the world. Don't get me wrong, me and Deleon don't really have problems in our relationship. His ass just don't trust me to do shit. It's been two years, and I have yet to be left alone with Faith.

It's like an unsaid issue in our house. If I brought that shit up, his ass would blow his fucking top. Instead of arguing about it, I enjoy my free time away from my family. Pulling up to my friend's house, I got out ready to

enjoy this last hour I had. Deleon and Faith would be

back to the house by then. After telling him I didn't have

anywhere to go, he would start the damn questioning.

Christa saw me coming and opened the door.

"Hey girl, I thought your ass wasn't gone make it.

Took your ass long enough." I met Christa at the gym,

and we clicked from the start.

"Bitch move, you out here acting like I got a lot of

time. You just wasted ten minutes trying to greet a

bitch. Now bring your ass on, and pour my drink." Yes, I

sneak and have a drink from time to time. A bitch had to

do it on the low because Deleon would probably leave

my ass if he knew. He thinks everything is an addiction.

"Your ass must have had a long day. What's going on with you and your forever fiancé?" This bitch knows she could throw shade when she wanted to.

"Me and Deleon good, and I been in the house all day. Just bored out of my mind, and need to relax. I'm trying to do some extra freaky shit tonight, so I need to be a little tipsy."

"Why haven't you pushed him on setting a date yet? Yall been together for what, four years now? You are letting that nigga string you along. For what? Because of Faith." This bitch was about to blow my buzz, and I just got the mother fucker.

"Look, I know you don't understand what me and Deleon have. It's not for you to get it, but we good. He has been more to me than you would ever know, and if

88

he needs a little time to make sure this is what he wants

to do, then I'm going to give it to him. Now pour me

another drink before I leave your ass here looking dumb

and bored." You could tell she had more to say, but she

better keep it to herself. I'm in the mood to hand out ass

whoopings and lollipops. Since a bitch ain't got no

lollipops, it will be more hands than anything. Downing

my last glass, I decided to leave anyway.

"I'll holla at you when you get all that hating out

your system. I'm not in the mood for all these questions.

I come over here to hang out with my friend, not get

interrogated by a bitch that can't hide her misery."

"Bitch please. Get over yourself. I'm your friend,

but friends know shit about friends. You be so damn

secretive; a bitch can't do shit but ask a million

questions. I'm sorry if you got offended, but I was just trying to have girl talk." Knowing my track record with friends were terrible, I may have come across a little strong.

"My bad. I've only had one friend and she slept with my man. I don't really know how to be girlfriends. My bad girl, but I need to get out of here before my baby gets home." Pouring a drink, I downed another glass and headed out the door. It would be a while before I had another drink, and I was glad I had a buzz going.

When I made it home, Deleon's car was at home. Fuck, he was about to trip and blow my buzz. Checking myself in the mirror, I tried to make sure there was no sign of my drinking on my face. After fixing my hair, I got out and headed in the house. Him and Faith were

playing the game, and they looked so content. The fact

that they were all into it, made me wonder how long

they been here.

"Hey baby, what do you guys want for dinner?"

They kept laughing as if my ass wasn't even in the room.

"Uh, hello. Mommy is home." Faith finally looked up and

ran to me.

"Hey mommy, I missed you. Come play with me

and daddy." She tried to pull me towards the couch, but

I needed to do my wifely duties.

"Baby, mommy has to cook. Maybe later." Deleon

grabbed me and kiss me, and my ass was ready to say

fuck dinner and go lay it on my man.

"Hey Del, I missed you daddy." He stared me in my eyes, and kissed me again. Walking away, he went back to the couch and started the game back up with Faith. Smiling, I went and started dinner. Grateful that the nigga didn't start questioning me about my whereabouts, I was about to hook his ass up one hell of a meal.

DELEON...

This girl must think I'm smoking with her ass. I knew Auri like I knew myself, and she was high off something. Her eyes glossed over whenever she had just a lil something. Mother fuckers thought I was just strict on her ass, but I been through too much to deal with

that shit again.

I went through hell and high water to get Auri

clean, and I'll be damned if I let her take me through

anything else like that. Don't get me wrong, Auri was

worth it. Not only was my baby beautiful, but she was

smart as hell. That nigga Sosa just had her going down

the wrong path. I was determined to save her, I needed

to save her, my heart had to save her.

Whenever I was around her, my soul moved. She

is my soul mate, but she came with a lifetime of

baggage. An addict will always be an addict, and my

trust issues were through the roof. Trying not to

smother her, I gave her as much space as my trust would

allow.

After my baby almost got killed under her watch, I didn't even allow her to stay with her alone. I know I was being extreme, but this was my family. Two years ago, I proposed to her at graduation. I'm sure Auri thinks I'm stringing her alone, but a nigga like me had to be sure we were done with this roller coaster ride. When I said I do, I wanted that shit to be forever. Auri ass was still moving suspect, and until I knew exactly what she was up to, I wasn't taking that next step.

At least that was my thought until recently. Lately, I been realizing how life is too short, and I didn't want to lose her. My wall has been up, and I know she feels it. My mama told me if I was going to be all in, then I needed to do the shit right. I got everything all planned out for Valentine's Day, to do it right. Now her coming in here all glossy eyed got me second guessing this shit all over again.

This was the ride I didn't want to be on, and the thought of her getting high again had me ready to kill her ass. It's not like she was a social smoker, her ass was a full-blown crack head. I know I had to let the shit go in order to move on, but I didn't know how. Just looking at her now, had me ready to beat her ass.

Taking Faith upstairs, I put her in the tub, so she could get ready for bed. Me and Auri needed to have a talk, and I didn't like to do that shit in front of her. After making sure she was good, I read her a story and headed out. Auri ass walked in the room like she didn't have a care in the world.

"Where the fuck you been?" I know she hated when I questioned her like this, but I needed to know why the fuck it looked like she been getting high.

"Don't talk to me like that. You can ask me a question without acting like I'm your damn child. I was with Christa, and the last time I checked, I was grown and could go outside." She was about to piss me off. Trying my best to stay calm, I took a breath before I responded.

"You act like I know this bitch. I've never met her, and I don't know what she about. You come in here looking like you high, and you mad because I'm asking where the fuck you been?"

"Asking is one thing, but you know what the fuck I meant. If you were going to condemn me for the rest of my life, why the fuck did you propose? Tell me Deleon,

why the fuck did you come back? This shit is stupid, and

if you don't trust me, maybe we need to rethink this

entire thing." Now I was fucking appalled.

"Oh, excuse the fuck out of me. I'm sorry, I may

have misread the situation. Let's see, I found you

cracked out sucking dick for money. Took you to rehab,

you got clean, got pregnant, and your ass got gone. You

went right back to that nigga getting high. I forgave you,

and trusted you with my child.

She almost lost her life, and let me think what you

did when you got out of jail. That's right, you went and

started back getting high. I got you clean again, and now

here we are. Did I leave anything out?" Standing there

speechless, I knew I had her ass stumped. "I didn't think

so." The moment she started crying, I felt like shit. I

wasn't trying to hurt her, I just needed her to

understand where my trust issues came from.

"Look baby girl, all I'm trying to say is don't act like

my trust issues aren't warranted. I'm not trying to make

you feel bad, or drag you through your past. I just need

to know that something won't set you off. I'm trying, it's

just hard and I'm sorry." Using my thumb, I wiped away

her tears. Pulling her into me, I was lost on how to get

her to see my point without hurting her feelings.

"I get it baby. I'm always going to be the

crackhead you saved. No matter what I do. Just know

I'm not getting high, and if you want to meet Christa you

can. It wasn't about hiding anything, but the one friend I

had slept with my man. Just know I'm dealing with shit

as well." Now a nigga was feeling like shit, but my point was still valid. Not knowing how to get through to her, I decided to leave it alone since I didn't want to hurt her any further. Deciding to take another route, I needed to relieve some stress.

"Put your pussy in my mouth baby." Just like that, I knew we were good. She started giggling, and I was about to tear that shit up. Sliding out her clothes, she ran to the shower. Laughing at her, I climbed in the bed. As soon as she was done, she climbed in the bed with no hesitation she sat on my face. Inhaling her scent had me hard as fuck.

Attacking her clit with my tongue, I slid my finger in her ass. That was the upside about her past, my baby was a freak.

"Mmm baby, I love the way you eat this pussy."

Sucking on her until she started shaking, the fingering

caused her to squirt all over me.

"Damn baby girl, you trying to drown my ass."

Pulling her down, I used the sheet to wipe my face.

Sliding her right on my dick, I was in the mood for her to

buck. On my lazy shit, I let her do all the work. With her

breasts bouncing with each flop, I gripped them bitches

and took over. Deep in her guts, I was tearing that shit

up.

"Quit trying to run Auri. Take this dick and I ain't

playing with your ass. Take this fucking dick."

"Aaaggghhhhhh fuck baby, it's too big. Slow

down, let me catch my rhythm."

"Fuck that, you gone catch this nut it's on the way up. You got me baby."

"Aaagghhh fuck." Making sure my balls were slapping her on the ass, I went as deep as her walls allowed.

"Daddy please stop hurting mommy." Looking up, we saw Faith at the door crying. Fuck. My baby was gone be scarred for life.

HANNAH...

Once again, Delow was MIA, and I had no idea where he was. I was tired of this shit, and I didn't put my all into someone for him to be cheating on me with some hood rat ass bitch. Valentine's Day was a month away, and I barely saw this nigga. That only mean one thing, he had some string beans on his plate. One thing I didn't tolerate was my man with a side chick. Picking up the phone, I called my mother because I needed some advice. This shit was hurting me to my soul, and I didn't know what to do.

"Hey ma, you busy?" She was a doctor, and I promise she never had time for me. Whenever I would complain, she would always say when I became a nurse I would see what she went through. That wasn't the case though. I made time for the people that was important.

"I got about ten minutes. Talk Hannah, I hate when you do that. You call, and then you beat around the bush." Every time I called her, she made me feel like I shouldn't have.

"It's Delow. Lately, he hasn't been coming home. It's like he is always preoccupied. I don't know what to do." You could tell she was half ass listening to me.

"First off, I told you not to date the street thug anyway. You are a nurse, and you deserve better. Second off, if he is not coming home then that's a good day for everybody. You deserve better, and wasn't he your ex boyfriend's homie anyway?" The way she said homie irritated me.

"I already know your stance on the matter, now can you help me? What am I supposed to do?"

"Be happy he isn't home. It's almost Valentine's Day, go out and find you a fresh new man. You don't need him. You are too good for a guy like him." Knowing this was a mistake, not even bothering to say goodbye, I hung up the phone. It's been this way my entire life. It was the only reason I became a nurse. Everything she wanted, anyone around her had to do it. She was demanding, and bossy. Not wanting to rock the boat, I did whatever she wanted.

Now here I am a grown ass woman, and I was still folding to everyone in my life. This shit was about to stop though, I didn't mind my man leading. Letting him do whatever the fuck he wanted, wasn't a part of that. I loved him, but I wasn't built for this.

Right as I was ready to throw his shit out, he came waltzing his ass in the door. Trying my best to ignore him, he came staggering over to me missing his attempt to kiss me on the mouth. He smelled like he been taking Henny shots with a needle.

"Hey baby you cooked? I'm hungry than a mother fucker." I wanted to put something in his mouth, but it wasn't no damn food. I was ready to slap his ass.

"I haven't seen you since yesterday morning, and you talking about some food. Go fix your own damn food."

"That's your problem, you always talking shit. Damn. Can a nigga breathe, I had shit to do. You act like I'm out here cheating on you. I do have an entire business to run. The streets ain't gone sell drugs they damn self." That was another thing, I really wish he would walk away. Deleon did, and handed it down to Delow, but he had enough to quit.

"You say that shit like it's normal. Your ass do not have to be out for days. That is something you are choosing to do. All I'm asking is for you to be here. If you don't want to be, then leave. I'm not doing this with you." This nigga was so fucked up he could barely hear me.

"I hear you baby, I will do better, now can we please stop arguing?" Grabbing me, he pulled me to the couch. Laying with him, at first, I was wondering about Valentine's Day. Now, I was worried about our future all together.

DELOW...

The truth is, I was avoiding being home with Hannah. All she wanted to do was talk about Valentine's Day, and that was the one thing I wanted to stay away from. This shit was tearing my soul, and I couldn't talk to her about it. How do you explain to your chick that the most important holiday to them, was one you would hate forever?

Sosa killed Jess and my baby right before Valentine's Day, and the shit was hitting me hard. If I could kill that nigga again, I would. The fucked up thing about all of it is, he didn't even want Jess. He killed her like she wasn't shit, just so he could keep Auri on crack.

I loved that girl, but she couldn't see me. A nigga that wanted her no matter who she was. I didn't give a fuck how many niggas she fucked, or what she did in her life. All I wanted was her, and all she wanted was him. The shit was a mess, but I was willing to be messy as fuck as long as she was in my life.

I didn't even know about the damn baby until the news reported it. I'm nobody's fool, and I know it was a possibility that the baby could be Sosa's. The fact that I don't care, is what scares me the most. How could I give my all to Hannah, when I was still stuck on my past?

Looking over at my baby, I felt like shit because it seemed like I was leading her on. Getting out of bed, I headed to the bathroom and attempted to freshen up. Throwing on my jogging suits, I grabbed my keys and headed out the door. Jumping in my whip, I drove with so much on my mind.

Pulling up to the cemetery, I sat in my car and pulled out my baggie. Sniffing as much coke as I could handle, I didn't get out of the car until I was fucking lifted. Finally able to pull myself out, I staggered towards the grave. I've been out here every day, and even though Hannah thought I was cheating, I wasn't. Well maybe to some, this was cheating. What I mean is, I wasn't sticking my dick in nobody else. My heart was just buried six feet under with my baby.

Sitting down next to the headstone, I laid there and just rubbed my fingers across her name. I still couldn't believe that he killed my possible seed. Hannah doesn't even want kids, she never talks about babies or being a mom. I loved her, but I still loved Jess.

Why the fuck did I have to be the one going through this shit? I was a good nigga. Yeah, my profession is debatable, but I treat women right. Yet, I always get fucked over. Looking over at the headstone, I got pissed.

"Why the fuck did you have to sleep with him? Why you couldn't see what you had in front of you. I loved your ass, and you treated me like shit. Do you even know who the father was? Is that why he killed you?" I always asked her a million questions, but I never got the answers I was looking for.

Pulling out another baggie, I sniffed some more coke. Whenever I came out here, I got lifted. Pulling out some Henny, I drunk some liquor straight from the bottle. Frustrated as fuck with no answers, I decided not to sleep here today.

Getting back in my car, I headed to Deleon's house. I needed someone to talk to, and he was the only homie I had. When I got to his house, I was happy as hell to see his car in the driveway. Getting out my whip, I knocked on the door.

"Hey D, you good nigga? You look bad." He was looking me over, and I could tell he was trying to figure out what was going on with me.

"Can we talk? Out here, I don't want Auri to know my business." A questioning look went across his face, but he walked out behind me. "It's around the time that Jess and the baby died. Hannah wants to celebrate Valentine's Day, and all I wanna do is get high. I've been sleeping at the gravesite most nights."

"You look like your ass two steps away from being in the gravesite with her. I'm not sure what you and her relationship was like, but I do know that it's not on you. She chose to chase behind that nigga, just like Auri. All we could do was try. You did what you could, she didn't

want that. I'm not telling you that it's wrong for you to

grieve, but don't die with her. You have to live. Drugs,

and this sad shit is not going to make you better. You

need help, and you are not going to find it at the grave

D."

Tears falling from my eyes, I knew what he was

saying was true. I've always did coke, but I had it under

control. Or so I thought. Since the death, it has gotten so

much worse. A nigga was falling off the deep end, and I

didn't know how to brace my fall. I still wasn't ready to

hear that I was an addict though.

"You got me fucked up, and if I didn't have to

report to you to run this city, I would beat the fuck out

of your goofy ass." This nigga actually laughed at me.

"Nigga, don't let that dope gas you up. It's just that nigga, gas. Let that shit out your mouth, or let it out your ass. Just don't let the shit get you killed. I'm trying to help your dumb ass, but I won't do this with you. I went through this shit with Auri, because my girl sucks a mean dick. You are replaceable." The high must have had me feeling froggy as hell because my dumb ass fucked up.

"You ain't gotta tell me nigga, I had her. Along with everyone..." That was all I got out, and this nigga hit me so hard I was on the sidewalk and a nigga hadn't touched a step. When I saw him coming towards me, I wish I had shut the fuck up and listened.

"Get the fuck up Red Bull." This nigga had jokes, but even if I wanted to, he had knocked the giggle out my ass. Nigga was talking shit cus I flew. Guess his bitch

ass trying to say I got wings. If I was sober, I would have

beat his ass. For now, all I could do was pray this shit

ended quick. How the hell I come over here for help, and

ended up helping my ass get knocked the fuck out.

When he saw I wasn't moving, his ass didn't stop to

think it was because I couldn't, he just assumed I was

being a hard ass.

Reaching down, he punched my ass so hard, my

ass was snoring before my eyes even closed. This can't

be life.

REASON NUMBER 4

"Took a little time for me to see, that girl I need you right here next to me. I could let you walk away, but baby I'm not going out that way. Cus I can't live without you, can't be without you. I'm begging you to stay. I love you, and even though I said that you could leave me. I wanted other chances to adore you. I still believe in you and me." I love you- Dru Hill

AURI...

This two weeks to Valentine's Day have flown by, but I wasn't happy about this shit one bit. Even though me and Deleon talked about the situation, he still was acting an ass. Not knowing what else to do, I took him to meet Christa. She all but threw herself at him. The bitch been calling me every day talking about how I need to get my shit together before he leaves me. How could I be stressed out when I got a nigga like him at home? Blah blah, fucking blah.

I couldn't even go over there and really drink in peace. Everything out of her mouth was about this nigga. Like damn bitch, I know everything about him, I mean, he is my nigga. She is acting like I just met him, and she has to convince me how much of a catch he is. If I didn't know that, I wouldn't be here. That man saved me, but a bitch still needed a break every now and again.

Grabbing my keys, I headed out the door to my parent's house. His ass been moving in secret this past week, and I don't like it. Ever since our argument, his ass been moving different. It's like he's here, but he's not at the same time. When he is around me, his touch is softer. His tone is more loving, it's like he is perfect. Then he leaves home, and I won't hear from him for hours. Damn near an entire day.

When he left a little while ago, he said he was going to stop by my parent's house. Then run some errands. I was about to do a pop up on this nigga. A bitch needed answers, and to see if his ass was lying. Leaving out, I jumped in my car and sped to my parent's. The first thing I noticed when I pulled up was, Deleon's car was nowhere in sight. Jumping out of my car, a bitch was pissed. All I wanted to do was beat his ass. Not

bothering to knock, I used my key to walk in.

"Hey baby, it's been a while since I saw you. How

you and Deleon doing?" My mother ran and hugged me

like it's been years since we saw each other.

"Mom, have Deleon been by here today? Have

you talked to him?" Her expression changed, and I knew

the answer.

"Oh baby. Did he leave you? What happened? We

haven't seen you, Faith, or Deleon in a couple of weeks."

Trying to fight back tears, I prayed we both were wrong

and maybe he talked to my dad.

"Where's dad?" You could see the sympathy in

her eyes, but I didn't give a fuck about that shit. Two

days out this week alone, he told me he was taking Faith

by my parent's house before he ran his errands. One of

those days, my ass was trying to get a drink, so I didn't

think anything of it.

"He's upstairs." Running upstairs, I screamed for

my dad to answer me. I could feel my world crumbling

with each step.

"I'm in here sweet pea." Running towards his

office, I prayed he would ease my mind.

"Hey dad, have you seen Faith and Deleon? Have

they been by here?"

"No baby, we been waiting to see grandbaby for a

couple weeks now. Quit holding her hostage, you know

we old and we don't have long. Damn shame how yall

keep that baby from us. Why does Deleon have to bring

her anyway? She is your child too, why can't you bring

her?" Trying to hold back the tears, I didn't want my parents to worry.

"Dad, you know what happened. He is still struggling with trusting me with her by myself. It's okay, I just wanted to know if she had been by here."

"That's the craziest thing I ever heard. If he doesn't trust you, why the hell did he come back? Tell him I said to bring my baby by here." Giving him a hug, I got ready to leave.

"I'll tell him dad." Walking down the stairs, I didn't even bother saying bye to my mom. The tears were fighting to fall, and I didn't want them to see me crying. As soon as I got in the car, I freed them as I headed to his moms. That was another place he claimed he had been going this week. I'm sure he had been here, because he always go to see his mom. When I pulled up, I noticed his car wasn't there either. Getting out, I was a bit calmer because I knew she had seen him. As soon as she opened the door, she hugged me.

"Hey Auri, you don't mess with me no more huh? I haven't seen you in a while. How's it going? Tell my son if he don't bring my baby by here to see me soon, I'm going to beat his ass."

"What?" Hearing that he hadn't been by here either shook me to my core.

"I said tell my son I'm going to beat his ass if he don't make his way over here. I'll keep her for Valentine's Day so you two can celebrate. It's not like I have a man." So many thoughts went through my head, but nothing would come out.

Finally snapping from my thoughts, I tuned back in to hear what she was saying. Her ass hadn't missed a beat and was still talking.

"I'll tell him ma. Let me get going so I can run to the store. I need to get dinner started in a little while."

"Okay baby. See you soon." Kissing her on the jaw, I left out of the house. Everything in my body screamed Auri get high. I was craving drugs so bad, my ass started shaking. Jumping in my car, I drove to the one place I knew would help me. I needed something, and I needed it bad.

When I pulled up, the first thing I noticed was Deleon's car. Nothing I could do would stop the tears from falling. My legs felt like bricks with each step that I took. Everything was dead silent, and I was in a zone.

Not even bothering to knock on the door, I tried the knob and it opened.

"Is this why you wanted to meet my friend?" The look on their faces were priceless. Christa jumped to her feet, but I stayed zoned in on Deleon.

"Auri, I promise it's not what you think. Let me explain." Not even bothering to look at Christa, I stared fire into my man.

"Is this why you wanted to meet my friend?" The look on his face read fear, but it wasn't him that needed to be worried. I was scared of what I would do to myself. Standing up, he tried to walk over to me, but I raised my hand to stop him.

"Auri, you know me. The fact that you are standing here questioning me is shocking as fuck. I went through hell for you. I walked away from someone that had done nothing wrong, when all you did was hurt me. All I wanted was you. Don't start having trust issues now." He was right, but that still didn't change the fact that he was here, and he had no business in this mother fucker.

"Besides, nobody wants you to relapse. Please calm down, we are not trying to get you worked up." Slowly turning my head, I looked at the bitch like she had two heads. Turning back towards Deleon, the look on his face said, 'I know I fucked up'.

"You told her my business."

"Auri."

"YOU TOLD HER MY FUCKING BUSINESS." Before he could respond, or she could see it coming, I lunged at her. Using all my pain, hurt, and disappointment, I fucked that bitch up. With each punch, she balled up screaming and crying. Not having an ounce of mercy, I plummeted her head with my fist, until Deleon pulled me from her. He thought his ass was safe until I punched his ass in the mouth. Standing still, he allowed me to attack him until I was tired. Walking towards the door, I could barely see from the tears.

"Just so you know, we are done. You're finally free of the crackhead. I hope you are happy now. Happy Valentine's day."

DELOW...

Looking around my room, I was having a bittersweet moment. Half of me was happy as hell to be getting out of this place, and the other half didn't want

to deal with the issues outside this place. Valentine's

Day was a couple of days away, and I still hadn't dealt

with my issues.

Deleon ass brought me to rehab, and they were

releasing me on today. My ass was knocked out cold,

and when I opened my eyes, I was here. The detox

wasn't pretty, but I was determined to kick that shit. My

emotions were already all over the place, and I didn't

need the drugs making it worse.

I felt like a new nigga now that I didn't have any

coke in my system. The shit is crazy how good your body

feels, once its detoxed from all the bullshit. Even though

I was feeling like new money, I was ready to get the fuck

from out of here. This place fucked with your mental,

and I had enough shit going on.

Grabbing my stuff, I looked around and headed

out the door. Knowing Hannah wouldn't be here to pick

me up, I could go by the cemetery. Deleon never told

her where I was, but he tried to talk me into doing it.

Not wanting her to know I was on drugs, I decided

against it. The only visitor I've had since I been here was

Deleon. That nigga knows he sholl don't mind saving a

crack head. When I walked outside, he was standing

there waiting.

"Damn nigga, I didn't expect anyone to be here to

pick me up. You solid as fuck." Climbing in the car, he

didn't drive off and I knew he wanted to talk.

"I've been down this road before, and I know how hard it is to stay clean. If you have no intentions on doing the right thing, don't go back to Hannah. Nobody deserves that kind of heartache." Feeling what he was saying, I knew me going to the cemetery was the right thing.

"I'm good. I appreciate everything man. For real. Even though I didn't feel like I was an addict, I know what that shit did to my body. I ain't trying to go back to that shit."

"That's what I'm talking about. If you feel like relapsing, call me nigga. No matter what time it is. I'll drop you off, so you and your girl can make up."

"Just take me to my car, I have somewhere else to go first." You could tell he didn't want to do that, but what choice did he have. I was grown as fuck.

"Daddy, I want mommy." My ass just realized Faith was in the car.

"Not today baby. How about ice cream instead?"

"Okay." This nigga over here giving me advice, and it seems him and Auri ass going through it they damn selves.

"What's going on with you and your girl? Trouble in paradise?" He was pissed I found humor in his situation.

"Trust issues. I was treating her like she was still an addict instead of just talking to her. Once I realized what I was doing to her, and our relationship it was too late. Now she don't trust me, and everything all fucked up. I'm going to fix it, because that girl is my damn world man. It was all a misunderstanding, but she doesn't know that. You think I'm in your business, I just don't want you to make the same mistakes I did. Do what you have to do to come to terms with your past, before you lose your future." He left me with those thoughts because we were now at my car. Nodding, I climbed out.

"Thanks for everything again. I appreciate it." Closing the door, I headed over to Jess's grave. This was the first time I came here sober. It felt different, and I didn't really know where to start. Taking a deep breath, I poured my soul out to the air and dirt hoping she would hear me.

"Jess, for the longest, you had me questioning why I wasn't good enough. Was it something wrong with me? If I had done shit differently, would you still be here? So many questions, with no answers. Half of the reason I couldn't let you go, is the guilt I felt.

If I had been a better man, would you have been here? Now that I'm sober, I realize I can't do that to myself. I can see now that I gave you everything and you shitted on my ass like I was nothing. You were a taker, and nothing I did would have ever made you happy.

You're still taking from me. I have a good woman at home, but I can't give her my all because you still have a hold on a nigga. I need to be better to her, because she doesn't deserve to only get half of me. I need you to let me go Jess." Wiping the tears from my eyes, I didn't feel any different. While I waited for a sign,

a feeling, hell something. I started to feel defeated.

Closing my eyes, I was starting to think maybe it wasn't

meant for me to have a happy ending. Opening my eyes,

I looked up, and it was a bunch of birds flying over us.

Then they flew off. Feeling like a weight was lifted off my

shoulder, I smiled.

"Thank you Jess." I don't know if she was sending

me a sign, but it was what I needed. I saw it as her telling

me to be free. Running towards my car, I had one more

stop to make. I had one shot to make it up to her, and I

planned on taking it.

A nigga didn't know much about Valentine's Day,

but I was determined to make it special for her. I know

Deleon had done enough for me, but I needed his help

one more time. That nigga was the king of romantic, and I needed his ass to pull off a miracle for me. His ass was gone have to tell me what to do to get my girl back. With him and Auri on the outs, I hoped he still had it in his ass.

AURI...

"All the time that I was loving you, you were busy loving yourself. I would stop breathing if you told me to, now you're busy loving someone else. Four God damn years out of my life, besides the kids I have nothing to show. Wasted my years a fool of a wife, I should have left your ass a long time ago."

My ass was screaming out the lyrics to Not Gon Cry by Mary J. Blige. I'm sure my parents wanted to tell me to shut the fuck up. I've been here ever since I caught Deleon cheating on me. Even though my mind was trying to push me over the edge, I refused to use another drug. I was so far from that place in my life, and it made me realize just how strong I was.

My ass was broken to pieces, I cried and brought my ass in the house. Don't get me wrong, I been crying ever since I been in this bitch, but I was crying sober. I loved Deleon too much to ever hurt him like that again. But I can damn sure sit my ass in here and curse his ass, and sing I hate you songs.

Tired of hurting, I cut the radio off and laid down. The music was only making it worse. A bitch heart was hurting, and I was done feeling like this. Tomorrow, I was getting my ass up and going outside. If this was the game Deleon wanted to play, I was gone figure out how to play it better.

His ass had me fucked up, and I was done with the games he wanted to play. I didn't tell his ass to save me, and I didn't tell him to take me back. These were all decisions he chose to make on his own. How the fuck he gone punish me and he the one out here choosing. Closing my eyes, I prayed for just a little bit of sleep.

The fire was burning through my soul in the worse way. I was shaking from the feeling that was being given to me. Knowing how much he hurt me, I should have stopped him. His tongue was making perfect circles around my clit, sending me into a high I have never felt.

When his lips wrapped around my clit, a whimper escaped my lips. My body was betraying my heart, and I didn't know how to stop it. The juices started flowing, and his fingers replaced his mouth. Once my body stopped shaking, I would tell him to get the fuck out. I needed him to go so I could think straight.

As I started to calm down, I got ready to curse his ass out, when his dick pierced my soul. He slid it in so swift all I could do was arch my back. With each stroke, he kissed my tears away. His hands brushed lightly over my nipples, as he made love to my mouth and pussy.

As if our bodies were in sync, he started to shake just as mine had a seizure. Everything about him turned me on, but as soon as we were done, the hate came back. Opening my eyes to curse his ass out, I looked around and I was in the room alone. The only sign that

let me know I wasn't crazy, and Deleon was actually

here, was his scent. I could smell Bond #9 throughout

the room. Sighing, I laid back on my pillow frustrated.

That nigga pulled a drive by on my ass. My heart hurt,

but at least my pussy felt great.

****

After showering and getting my hygiene together,

I got dressed and headed downstairs. Yeah that nigga

had my pussy singing love songs last night, but I was still

on a mission today. He couldn't just fuck me and make

everything okay. He had me fucked up if he thought I

was the same weak ass Auri he met years ago.

"Hey ma, I'll be out all day, but I will be back later.

I would appreciate if you give me a heads up the next

time you're going to let Deleon in." Her old ass started

blushing like she knew what we had done last night.

"He wanted to talk to you." We did absolutely no

talking. "Give him a chance baby. I'm sure you are over

reacting. You've always been that way." Now I was

pissed.

"Mom you do not know what happened? No, you

don't. Please just let us handle this. What do you have

planned for today?"

"I had mother daughter day planned for us, but it

seems like all you want to do is be away from me." I

could tell she was trying to guilt trip me. She knew the

shit was going to work.

"Are you ready? Come on, we can hang out." The

smile spread across her face.

"Yup, I'm ready." Grabbing her purse, we headed out of the door. I had no idea what she wanted to do today, but I hope it was men around.

"Where are we going ma?" You could see the nervousness on her face, and I knew it was about to be some bullshit.

"Can we swing by the church first?" I know her ass didn't just say church. Aw hell naw.

"Ma, no not today."

"Baby, I just want the pastor to say a quick prayer over you. I know you think everyone doesn't trust you, but I do. I just want God to continue to give you the strength you need. You're so strong, is it so wrong for me to want it to stay that way?" The tears started to fall down her face, and I knew my ass was about to be in church. I should have stayed my ass in the bed. Everyone

thought I was this fragile ass person. Her ass was praying

I didn't relapse, and wanted some extra help. If this

could help us get our day started, then fine.

Pulling into our church parking lot, I prayed

service wasn't long today. I wasn't properly dressed, and

I know my mama was gone try to get me to this alter.

Rolling my eyes, I snatched my purse and walked inside.

I had the worst luck in the world. How in the hell did

Valentine's Day fall on bible study day? I was trying to be

in the mall or something getting me a fuck him girl dress.

Tonight, I was going to be spending Valentine's Day with

somebody. I'm sure Deleon and Christa was going to be

spending it together.

Stepping inside, I froze when I saw all the decorations. Everything was red, and white. The tears got ready to fall as I realized I would not be spending today with Deleon. Everyone was seated already, and I tried to slide in the back. Of course, my mama pushed me towards the front. When I say the front, I mean the front. Our ass was sitting front row.

If I could curse her ass out, I would. Got me front and center with all these ugly ass decorations. Okay, they weren't ugly, but my ass didn't want to see this shit. Why the hell was the church celebrating this shit anyway?

"From the first time, I saw your face. Girl I knew I had to have you. I wanted to wrap you with, my warm embrace. Visions of your lovely face." I stood up shocked

as Let's Chill by Guy started to play on the speakers.

What the hell. Looking around the church, I just realized

our family was here. His mama, my dad, Christa, Hannah

and everyone else I could think of.

"All my love is for you. Whatever you want I will

do. You're the only one I want in my life. For you I'll make

that sacrifice." Deleon appeared out of nowhere

wearing an all white tux, with a red bow tie. It wasn't

until that moment, I realized everyone was dressed in

white. When he walked up to me, my heart stopped as

he got down on one knee.

"Auri, two years ago I proposed to you and you

said yes. I've been so caught up in the what ifs, and

maybes that I forgot about the right now. The first time I

laid eyes on you, I knew I was going to marry you. I've

been so selfish, and caught up in my own feelings, I

never took yours into consideration.

I'm sorry for having your family and my mama lie

to you. Some may think I was crazy, but it was my way of

showing you that, in the midst of another breakdown, or

life's obstacle I knew you would stay strong. That was

my way of showing you I had total faith and trust in you.

I'm sorry for ever making you cry, but I did all of that just

to get you to this moment.

On this Valentine's Day, I'm asking you to have

me. I trust you with my life, my soul, but most

importantly, with my heart. Will you marry me, today?"

My ass was so busy crying, I forgot to answer him. I

don't know how much time passed, but I could see the

worried looks on everyone's face including Deleon.

Getting down on my knees with him, I looked him into his eyes. Damn I loved this nigga.

"Yes." Kissing me, he pulled me to my feet.

"This is your wedding Auri. Go in the back your dress, and make-up artist is in there. Faith is being dressed right now, and all you have to do is walk down the aisle and say I do." Kissing him again, I ran to the back so I could marry the love of my life.

HANNAH...

This shit was just too damn beautiful for me. Deleon's proposal had me hating his ass all over again. Don't get me wrong, I'm over my feelings for him, but damn. Do this nigga just have to shit on every other bitch in the world. He just have to let us know how

we're settling for a piece of shit ass nigga. Speaking of

piece of shit ass niggas, mine disappeared on my ass a

month ago and I haven't heard from him.

No explanation, nothing. After he left that

morning, the nigga just didn't come back. It hurt like

hell, but maybe it was for the best. I would rather him

leave me, than to treat me like I ain't shit and cheat on

me. I'm not the type of bitch that will sit by and allow

that.

Trying my best to hold back the tears, I got my shit

together as the music started playing. Deleon was

standing at the front, and his ass looked nervous as hell.

Sexy than a mother fucker, but scared nonetheless. Faith

came walking down the aisle with an all white dress on,

and the shit was so sparkly it looked like it had real

diamonds on it. She smiled as she threw the red rose

petals. When she got to the end, she ran to her dad and

jumped in his arms. It was the cutest damn thing I ever

seen. The song changed, and Auri appeared at the door.

Everyone stood to their feet, and her ass was stunning.

She even took my damn breath away.

"My head's under water, but I'm breathing fine.

You're crazy, and I'm out of my mind. Cause all of me,

loves all of you." John Legend's All of me played, and

Auri ass was crying hard as hell walking down the aisle.

She must have known that was going to happen,

because there was no makeup on her face. As soon as

Deleon saw the tears, his ass started crying. Hell, I don't

think it was a dry eye in the room.

****

Now I'm no hater, but this wedding was just too much. The perfect guy, on the perfect day, and everything about it was just perfect. I'm sure she will never forget this Valentine's Day. As for me, I won't forget this mother fucker either. This was the worst day of my life, outside of witnessing the most perfect wedding ever.

Auri, Deleon, and Faith waved to us as they rode off on a horse and carriage. Getting in my car, I started to skip the reception, but I knew I couldn't do that. It's just hard watching somebody so in love, when your heart is hurting so bad. When I pulled up, I headed inside hoping this shit would be over soon.

They announced the newlyweds, and everyone laughed as they danced all the way to their table. They looked so happy, and you couldn't do shit but smile at their ass. This was not how I planned on spending Valentine's Day, but it would have been easier if I had a man here.

Everyone took their seat, and Deleon hit his glass to get everyone's attention. My ass wasn't gone be able to take much more of this shit. Feeling like I wanted to throw up, I prayed it stayed down today.

"Valentine's Day is a day for love, but all love isn't perfect. Sometimes, you have to go through Hell to find your Heaven. When you find your soul mate, it's not about finding someone that's perfect. It's about finding that person that's perfect for you." The nigga nodded towards the back, and everyone including me turned

around. There stood Delow, in his all white looking like a

damn snack. I was pissed at him, but it was hard not to

be horny at the same time. Walking towards me, he

spoke into the mic he had in his hand.

"No matter how much love a person gives you, it's

hard to receive it when you don't love yourself. I've

been abusing myself for years, not even realizing what I

was doing to myself. Hannah, I couldn't love you like you

wanted until I got my life together. You didn't want me

like I was, or I would have never been able to give you

my all.

I wasn't with another woman, I was in rehab. Not

only cleansing myself from all the bullshit I put in myself,

but to heal from old hurt. I'm ready to be not just the

man you want me to be, but I'm ready to be the man that you need me to be. What you see is what you get Hannah. A scarred, ex druggie, fucked up nigga that's in love with you. If you willing to love me with all my faults, I'm willing to give you my all. Hannah." My man dropped to his knees and pulled out a ring.

"Yes. Yes. Yes." Screaming, I didn't even give him the chance to ask me the question. Running towards him, I jumped in his arms.

"I hope he was about to ask you to marry him." Deleon joked in the mic, and everyone laughed.

Taking our seats, we went on with the rest of the reception. Valentine's Day ended up being the happiest day of my life as well. Now I could make it the same for him. Looking over towards him, he was already staring

at me just smiling. I was about to make his day better.

"You know, you're not the only one with a gift."

You could see the confusion on his face.

"What you talking about? You didn't have to get

me anything." Making him wait for a little while longer, I

just stared at him smiling.

"You're going to be a daddy." I knew he would be

happy, but I didn't realize it would affect him like this.

He started crying. Looking up to the ceiling, he smiled

with tears streaming down his face.

"Thank you Jess." When he turned back to me, he

kissed me passionately. "Happy Valentine's Day baby."

MY HOOVER

VALENTINE

REASON NUMBER 5

"What gave you the silly idea, that I'm about to leave. Girl who you been listening to, they must be crazy. Look back and see our past, and all the shit that we been through. I be damned if I let this bull crap take me away from you. Cus I vowed to give my all, and girl I'm a man of my word." I'll never Leave- R. Kelly

BABY FACE...

Juicy ass was walking around the house naked. She knew I couldn't resist her ass, and I had to get to this meeting with my brothers. My baby didn't want me to go, and she knew ass was a good way to damn near keep me here. Not this time though. We had too much to plan. From my mama's wedding, and Valentine's day, shit was a bit hectic. They ass wasn't giving us no room to breathe.

"Juicy go put some clothes on. That shit ain't working today. We got too much shit to do, and you know how Shadow is about us being late. Nigga will lecture for hours."

"Come on baby, just put the tip in. You know Tsunami wants me, I don't know why you choosing to keep him from me." My dick jumped, and I knew I had to get out of here fast before I lost this battle.

"I'll be back soon. Be naked for me, and make sure Zaria's ass is sleep. I'm not trying to be doing that sneak fuck, with your leg barely lifted." Laughing, she went in the bathroom. Knowing that was the only chance I would have to get the fuck out of there, I grabbed my keys and ran down the stairs. Heading out the door, I jumped in my Hummer driving to the main house.

My mama was planning her wedding, and she was driving all of us crazy. We were trying our best to still plan the shit we had for our girls, but my mama was making this shit hard as hell. She was doing the fucking most, and acting like her wedding was the revolution and it needed to be televised.

Pulling up, I jumped out because I was a few minutes late. That nigga really did the most about time, and that argument was only gone keep me away from my pussy longer. It took a while for me and Juicy to get back to this point. We did counseling, and that shit actually helped. After the baby, I barely got a glimpse of the pussy, let alone able to hit it. Depression is real, and her ass was driving me crazy. We were solid now, and I had my best friend back. My lil girl was still a damn cry baby though, and every chance she got her ass was cock blocking.

When I walked in the door, Quick and Blaze were wrestling. These niggas were some grown ass kids. Not wanting to get in the middle of the bullshit, I stood back and watched they ass. Throwing ad- libs here and there.

"Elbow his ass Quick. Swoop his leg Blaze." They both started laughing and walked towards me. Keeping my eye on Blaze, his ass play too much and I had to make sure he ain't do nothing stupid. Nigga was too old to still play the way that he do. You would think he would have grown up by now. I have no idea how the

fuck Drea puts up with him, and Spark.

"Keep instigating bitch it's gone get real hot in this

bitch." Knowing he was serious, I ignored his ass.

"Where the fuck is Shadow?" This nigga was never

around, and when we did see him his ass wouldn't say

shit.

"Been calling his ass all day, the nigga wouldn't

pick up. I know we let that shit slide because it was

Christmas, but this nigga moving real suspect. Yall better

get his dumb ass before I have that nigga looking like a

crispy Starburst." That nigga looked for any reason to set

somebody on fire. Most people would think he was

playing, but Blaze ass would do it.

"For once in your life can you think about something other than setting somebody on fire? Damn, it's other shit more important. Our brother could be in some shit, and that's the only thing on your mind. Grow up." Quick loved trying him, but I was nobody's fool. Blaze shut up, and I knew that meant nothing but trouble. His ass was up to something.

"Anyway, so about Valentine's Day. Where are we with the plans? Are they going to let us rent out the Island?" The entire purpose of the meeting, was to solidify the plans for the girls.

"Fuck no, your bald-headed ass mama wants to do her wedding on Valentine's Day. She just called this morning talking shit while her and the preacher was fucking, I hung up on her ass." She was losing her mind.

That wasn't happening. I'm surprised Blaze let her off

that easy.

"Well, I guess we are moving the meeting to her

house. She got this shit twisted." Grabbing our stuff, we

got ready to walk out.

"Why we got this big ass picture of Blaze still up in

the main house? We can paint this shit back white now.

we see his ass every day." I never thought about it until

Quick just said something.

"Nigga because I died. When you die you can get a

soul-glo memorial. Until then, shut your greasy ass up.

My ass was dead for months and his uglass questioning

my picture. Bitch I should put one up in all yall house. it

was your fault I died. Walk your shiny ass outside"

Laughing, we jumped in my truck and headed to see my

mama ignorant ass. Blaze be dead ass serious talking about he died. His ass was barely sleep, let alone dead. This was the best part about my life, only person missing was Shadow. Wondering what the fuck my brother had his ass mixed in, I was determined to get to the bottom of it.

BLAZE...

On the way to my mama's house, the car was quiet. We all were thinking the same thing, but nobody wanted to speak on it. Shadow's ass was into something, but we couldn't figure out what. If he was cheating on free Willy, he would have told us. My brother and them tried to ignore the shit like Kimmie ass wasn't around here looking like a pot of cheese grits, but I couldn't.

That baby had her ass thick as hell. I talked shit, but I

wasn't about to play with her ass. She might fuck my ass

up. Whenever I crack a joke, she looks like she be ready

to square up. My ass be nervous trying to find that Bic

fast as hell.

When we pulled up to my mama's house, I hoped

the pastor wasn't here. His ass always looking at us like

he trying to save our souls, when he is marrying the

worst of us. How Debra ass about to be somebody's first

lady was beyond me.

Walking in the house, mama was sitting on the

couch in a robe with no wig on. Her ass looked like a

silky spider. When she heard us laughing, she jumped up

from the couch.

"Why the fuck yall always sneaking in my shit. You could have warned a bitch you was coming over, so I could put my wig on." She walked over to a stack of boxes, and pulled out a wig.

"Ma, I know all those boxes ain't filled with wigs? The fuck you gone do with all them mother fuckers?" Her loony ass smiled, while me and my brothers looked at each other.

"I'm trying to pick the perfect one for my wedding day, and I just couldn't choose. Maybe yall can help me. Okay, I have this one what yall think?" Her ass pulled out this balled up ass wig. Mother fucker looked like a fist. She put it on her head, and we fell out laughing.

"Mama, that shit look like a wet dog. We gone call your ass poodle Hoover." She cut her eyes at Quick, and threw it back in the box. When she pulled out the next one, I was really in tears. This one was white.

"The young girls wearing grey and white weave, so I thought I would slay like they ass." When she put that one on, I was ready to leave.

"Man, your ass look like George Washington. If you don't get your Land of the free looking ass out of here. If I saw you in this hair, the only thing I would want to do is ask for a dollar." Baby Face was trying to stop me, but that shit looked bad. "You just gone be in your wedding stand there looking like Mount Rushmore huh? Throw that shit back in the box."

She was mad as hell, but we couldn't stop laughing. Snatching the next wig out, she gave us a look like we better not say shit. I couldn't talk if I wanted to.

It was a fake braided wig with beads on it.

"If yall don't like this one, yall some haters. When

I put this bitch on, mother fuckers gone know I'm Debra

Hoover."

"Naw ma, that mother fucker gone scream I'm

Rick James bitch. I'm not coming to your wedding, your

ass aint' about to make a fool out of me. In here looking

like a box of tricks, and I hope you gone get waxed. It's

your wedding, and that shit just nasty." You could tell

she wanted to whoop my ass.

"Fuck you bitch, I know somebody like it. Matter

fact, get yall simple ass out of my house. How the fuck

yall gone insult me in my shit. I'll look good in all them

bitches. I'm gone change a wig every hour, and I bet I

can have all the niggas trying to get in this tiger." I

couldn't stop laughing, so Baby Face tried to talk to her.

"Okay ma listen, you can't have your wedding on

Valentine's Day. We all have wives, and they ain't having

that shit. You can wait a couple of days, and do it that

Saturday. If you wait until Saturday, you can have

anything you want."

"I want a Bentley, and the bitch better be out

there after my wedding with a big fucking bow on it.

Now get the fuck out of my house, before I beat yall ass.

Disrespectful ass niggas."

"I was ready to leave anyway. It smells like two

booty cheeks clapping in this bitch." Not wanting to hear

shit else from us, she walked out and headed upstairs to

her room. My brothers started walking out the house,

but I eased over to the boxes. Reaching in my pocket, I pulled out my lighter and flicked my Bic. Them wigs must have had good chemicals on it, them bitches caught fire quick. Running out the door, I jumped in the Hummer fast as hell.

"Drive off, hurry up." Pulling out my phone, I texted my mama and let her know her living room was on fire. I ain't want her to go to sleep and not know them wigs were crispy.

"What the fuck you do?" Face was looking for an answer, so he didn't move.

"Nigga, drive. Mama about to beat my ass. Issa Cajun." Quick started laughing, but he didn't know I had something special planned for his ass. He wanted to talk shit, so that nigga was about to have one smoky Valentine.

"You set her house on fire? What the fuck is wrong with your ass?" Face always seemed shocked behind the shit I did.

"Naw dummy. Why would I set mama house on fire? I lit the fuck out of them wigs though." Everybody shook their head as we got the fuck out of there. I was gone have to buy her something special, and stay the fuck out of her way. She was gone fuck me up.

DREA...

Pacing the floor, I been waiting on Blaze to bring his ass back in the house. For the past two weeks these mother fuckers been disappearing, and that could only mean one thing. They ass was back in the business. Call me cocky, but I knew my nigga wasn't cheating on me. I put it the fuck down, and his ass was gone off this pussy.

The only other thing that makes sense, is that they are back in business. We all agreed that we were leaving that life in the past. If they thought for one second, we were letting that shit fly they were wrong. While they were having meetings, we were having meetings of our own.

"I don't know why yall think you too good to be cheated on, but you need to get over yourselves. These niggas leaving all times of the day, coming back smelling like perfume and shit. Hell, mine ain't been home for a single holiday. That ain't no business meeting, that's another woman. Juicy pass me some of that chicken."

Kimmie was trying to get us riled up, and I didn't like

that shit.

"I get that you're pregnant and pissed, but don't

bring that shit over here. I don't have those insecurities,

and I don't plan to start. Now if you want to sit at home

all day thinking your nigga inside another bitch's guts,

that's on you. My shit is laced, and my nigga gone."

"Bitch bye, you slept with his brother. I'm sure the

pussy is good, you had family sampling the shit. Let's be

real, do you ever think he would fully get over that?"

Now the bitch was crossing the line.

"If you weren't nine months pregnant, I would lay

your big ass out. You don't get to use that as an excuse

to be an asshole. Your nigga the only one been known to

cheat, keep it cute bitch. Real cute." You could tell Juicy

felt the same way I did, she looked like she was ready to

beat Kimmie's ass.

"You bitches crossing a line, but I'm with Drea on

this one. Quick ain't going nowhere. I know my nigga,

and that nigga ain't about to dip in another pussy. More

than likely, they back in the life. That shit is fucked up as

it is. Last time we barely made it out, and I don't want to

go through that shit again." That's why Ash was my

bitch. We thought alike.

"First off, I don't take ass whoopings. Pregnant or

not. Second, Ash please. Get off your high horse. The

reason you kept Zavi from him was because he cheated

with your home girl. I hear Drea's pussy is loose, maybe

he over here with her." That bitch tried it. Running

towards her, I was snatched in the air. The person was too strong to be one of these hoes, so I knew Blaze brought his ass home.

"Loosy gone upstairs before your ass end up in jail. Kimmie you gotta get your big ass up out my house. Where the fuck my couch go? You ate my couch? Tell your nigga when you see him, he owe me some furniture. His big ass whale done sucked down my shit." Blaze always had to do the most, but this time she deserved it.

"Fuck you. I'm not the bad guy, bitches just don't want to hear the truth. You smell good Blaze, what's that? Chanel number five."

"Naw, it's smoky six. Get the fuck out of my house Kimmie before I forget you my sister in law. You being real extra right now. In here acting like a two piece with

too many sides. You get side. You get a side. Everybody

gets a side." This nigga did not know when to shut up.

"Bye." She walked her mean ass out the house

with a plate of chicken. I couldn't do shit but laugh.

Knowing it was hormones, and fear, how do you be mad

at that. Well, she almost caught these hands, but still.

"I'm gone too. Kimmie ass ain't invited to the next

girl's day until she has that baby. I'm not gone be so

gracious next time." Juicy hugged me, and headed out.

Ash got up right behind her, and left.

Not only was it not a success, but we got our ass

caught. Now they ass knew we were up to something.

Hopefully, he didn't hear the entire conversation.

"Baby Spark is sleep, and I could use some of that shit, you gone give me daddy dick?"

"Your ass ain't slick Loosy, we gone talk about what the fuck all that shit was about, but you can suck this dick tho." Crawling over to him, you could tell he was turned on. The nigga dick damn near came out of his pants. "Let's fuck on the stove?" This nigga done lost his damn mind. If he thought I was gone let him put me that close to some fire, he had me fucked up.

"Nigga quit trying to act like you got millennium dick, when you slinging old man river. Don't be trying to do no new shit."

"Baby why you scared? I got you. Have I ever let you get caught on fire?"

"Fuck yeah you have. I'm scared because I ain't waxed this week, and I don't want my ass to catch fire. You know I be having some loose hairs back there. Let's go on the porch or something." This nigga laughed at me.

"How you scared of the fire when you married to Blaze? Get your scary ass in the kitchen. I ain't say shit about turning the mother fucker on. Come on baby." Knowing I needed to take my ass to a bed, I followed daddy in the kitchen. Picking me up, he placed me on the stove. Pulling my pants down, he pushed my legs all the way back and attacked my pussy.

"Yaaassssss daddy. Yassssss eat that shit." My body started to shake. That orgasm was coming so strong, my ass cheeks were shaking. Pulling me to the edge, I damn near passed out when he pushed inside

me. "Damn baby, you brought dick too. I ain't know you

brought dick too."

"Don't play with me, I always bring dick. Now shut

your ass up and take this shit." Doing what daddy said, I

took that shit. Throwing that shit back, my juices were

flowing down my leg. I could feel him all in my guts. Fuck

what the fuck Kimmie was talking about, that nigga

know he couldn't get this gushy shit from nowhere else.

Out of nowhere, my ass started getting hot.

"Nigga, why the fuck did you turn the fire on? Let

me up." My ass hairs were catching fire quick.

"Baby, I ain't turn shit on. Aww hell. Spark, get

your ass out of here." He was so busy trying to get Spark

out of here, that nigga forgot to turn the fire off.

Jumping down off the stove, I knew my damn ass cheeks were fucked up. This was why I shouldn't have brought my ass in here. Him and his daughter could kiss my scathed ass.

Running upstairs I ran some cold water, and tried to soak my ass. that shit was hurting too bad, so I got my ass out. Trying to rub some ointment on my shit, I was in tears trying to get that shit on.

"Damn Loosy, she fucked your ass up. Let me see." Pushing him back, I didn't want him anywhere near me. He played too damn much. When he grabbed the ointment, I gave in and let him help me. The shit hurt like all hell, and I had tears in my eyes. Rubbing the oil on me gently, my baby took care of me.

"This shit better be healed by Valentine's Day. I ain't fucking no spotted meat." My ass should've known it wouldn't last long.

SHADOW…

Packing my bag, I left the lady I was with as she was. Heading out the door, I knew I needed to get home. My brothers and them tripping, and this shit is becoming harder to hide. I know I should be focused on my wife, and the baby that is about to be here any day now, but I had to keep my head in the game.

None of they ass would understand that this is what I needed to do. All the fuck they would do is judge the fuck out of me, and I wasn't with that shit. Even though I'm the baby, I'm grown as hell. Kimmie and me stayed arguing, and this shit was starting to put a strain on our marriage.

I wish I could tell her what was going on, but it was against the rules. Gangsta was very clear on what I could and couldn't do, and that was one. After working with him, and seeing how he got down first hand, there was no way I would go up against his ass. The nigga was certified crazy, and I was in training to be just like him.

When I walked in the office, he was there waiting on me. My nigga had my back, and he would never go back home until I was done with training for the day. It was hard for me to talk to him about my personal problems, because he really didn't give a fuck. Trying my luck, I decided to see if he would make an exception.

"What up G? You know my brothers are going to fuck me up for missing the meeting today, and don't get me started on the argument I'm about to have with Kimmie's ass." He nodded in agreeance.

"You don't have to tell me, I've been down that road, and don't want to go back."

"I was wondering if you could make sure I have Valentine's Day open. My ass done missed Christmas and all, but if I miss that day, Kimmie is going to kill me." You could tell he was unbothered by my request.

"Did I ever tell you how I became a hit man?" Shaking my head no, he continued his story. "You already know the story of me and Paradise cutting up my parents. Well, Suave walked in on us and that fucked with his mental.

My brother, the only nigga I had left in this world brought me a million dollars, and basically told me to get the fuck on. Said I was becoming a liability. That was the day I turned off the last part of my emotions. That was the day Lucifer was fully born. Me and him didn't speak or see each other for ten years.

I said all of that to say this. In this life, you are going to lose some people along the way. I'm not talking about fake ass friends, or mother fuckers you don't care about. The life we live takes away family, friends, kids, and wives. I was one of the lucky ones, because mine is just like me.

There will come a time where you will have to choose them, or this life. I hope you are ready to make that decision. If not, the powers that be will make the decision for you." After the nigga said all of that, I still didn't have my answer about Valentine's Day. As if he could read my mind, he answered.

"I'll see what I can do, but there are no guarantees. Me and my crew will be here on that day, and I plan on spending it with my wife. If duty calls, my wife will understand. Go home and be with your girl." Not feeling any better, I walked out the door and headed home. This was about to be a long night, but if I missed Valentine's Day, she was going to hate me forever.

Just because I had to cut my feelings off, doesn't mean she had to suffer. Kimmie didn't sign up for this, and I hate that I switched it up on her after we got married. I'm supposed to be retired, and at home living the good life. Instead, my ass sneaking around just to train with this nigga.

Don't get me wrong, this was a decision I made on my own. It was something I had to do for me. A nigga got tired of living in my brother's shadow. Nobody feared me, they feared my brother's and our last name. To everyone besides my brothers, I was a joke. G made me realize that the first time we met. Calling me a purse dog and shit.

Even though this shit getting hard, I promised him that I would take this shit serious. That's what I was doing, so no matter how pissed my girl was, I had to see this shit through. Before I went home, I stopped by Baby Face house to see what happened at the meeting. Quick would have an attitude, and Blaze would do the most.

Even though I had a key, I rang the bell. I ain't want to walk in on some shit, that I couldn't unsee. You could see the disappointment on his face, when he realized it was me.

"Nice of you to finally show the fuck up. The meeting was hours ago Mr. My time is money. Where the fuck you been?"

"I had an errand to run. So, what we decide on?" Shaking his head, I knew he wasn't gone let it go that easy.

"Nigga, it seems like all you do is run errands. We didn't get shit done because we had to go by mama house. She was trying to have her wedding on Valentine's Day, but we shut it down. It's going to be the

Saturday after. You better not miss your mama's

wedding."

"I won't, but I may have to miss Valentine's Day.

My ass being pulled in every direction and I don't know

what to do. I love Kimmie, but I may have to let her go."

His face went from disappointed, to disgusted.

"Nigga are you crazy? Whatever you are doing out

there in them streets, it's not worth you fucking up your

home over it. Matter fact, your bull shit starting to pour

over into our house. Your girl trying to plant seeds and

shit that all of us are cheating and shit. You need to get

your shit together."

"I'm trying, and everything will make sense in the

end, but for right now, I have to do this."

"DO WHAT NIGGA? Nobody knows what the fuck you are doing. It's all of us, or none of us. You breaking code my nigga. We can't save you, or help you if you don't tell us what the fuck is going on." Now I was pissed.

"That's the point, I don't need yall to save me. I got this. I'm not baby Shadow anymore running up behind you niggas. That's what's pissing you off ain't it? Tell the truth. Quick always been a killer by instinct. It was his thing, to be the shooter. Yall scared of Blaze. The only way for yall to stay feeling like that nigga in the streets is to run over me, or have me at your beck and call. Those days are over my nigga. Worry about your shit, and I'll worry about mine." Walking out, I slammed the door in his face. Cutting off anything further he might have wanted to say.

When I got home, I was still pissed. It would be in Kimmie's best interest if she just let a nigga be tonight. As soon as I walked in the door, I realized my luck wasn't that great. She threw a shoe at my ass, and I was ready to lay her big ass out.

"You think you can walk in and out my house when you fucking feel like it? Nigga you can get your shit and get the fuck out." Laughing, I had to make light of the shit, before I hurt her fucking feelings. "Oh, you think it's funny? You got ten seconds to get the fuck out of my shit."

"First of all, this my shit. Second, I'm not in the mood for your depressing ass bullshit. Third, I'm horny.

If you want to do something with your mouth you can come suck this dick." When the tears welled up in her eyes, I felt bad. Knowing I couldn't show it, it hurt my heart to know she thought I didn't give a fuck. That was the first thing G taught me. I had to turn off my emotions if I wanted to protect her.

Instead of going to her, and telling her how much she meant to me, I walked to the bathroom to take a shower. My mind was in a million places. I understood what G was teaching me, and I didn't want him to think I didn't appreciate the training he was giving me. However, I wasn't that nigga that was into hurting his girl.

My brothers think I'm being disloyal, and my girl think I'm cheating. I never thought I would have to give up one life, to live another. Somehow, some way, I had

to figure out how to fix this. One thing was for certain, I

couldn't miss Valentine's Day, or she was going to kill

me.

DEBRA...

Yasss bitch yasssss. Blaze had me fucked up. He

thought burning my wigs was gone stop my show. A

bitch got her an express shipment, and I had some new

wigs. Each one I tried on spoke to my life, and I had to

pick which one I was going to wear.

Hell, I just may wear them all. That's how a bitch

was feeling. Like changing it up every hour. I might

change my shit right at the fucking alter.

"Baby, what are you in here doing?" Spinning around in the mirror, I turned to face my fiancé.

"Trying on wigs for my big day. Where you been?"

"I had a meeting with Sister Thomas, trying to get the program done right. I know you want your day to be perfect."

"Nigga if you want to see that day, your ass better stay away from that hoe. I'm not gone tell your ass again. That bitch wants you, and I don't have no problems tapping that ass. Try me if you want to."

"Baby she is sixty years old. What am I going to do with her? Most of the time her ass need a cane to walk. You need to stop that jealous mess. Once you are first lady, you are gone have to work with everybody."

"Just because she sixty don't mean her cat don't purr. It just means that mother fucker yawns first, and how many times do I have to tell your ass I'm not being no damn first lady." His ass had the nerve to sigh like I was getting on his nerves.

"We will work on that after you say I do. First things first. Why aren't you dressed, I told you that we needed you to be baptized before we go through with this wedding." I see he was determined to fuck my day up.

"Nigga I take a bath every damn day, and if God sees all, he saw my ass in that water. Boom, I was baptized. Now get the fuck on, so I can finish trying on my shit."

"No Debra. I bend on a lot of stuff, but if we are going to get married, I need you to be baptized. Get dressed and let's go. We have thirty minutes before we start." Seeing that this argument wasn't going anywhere, I decided to teach him a lesson. Ain't no forcing me to do something when I don't want to. He was about to learn this shit the hard way.

****

"Take me to the water. Take me to the water. Take me to the water, to be baptized." The church sung, as I walked towards the baptism pool.

"Nothing but the righteous. Nothing but the righteous. Nothing but the righteous, shall see God." Stepping in the water, I was mad as hell this shit was cold.

191

"Your ass knew all day you were bringing me here and your ass couldn't warm the water up?" Everybody gasped, and I didn't see why. They should be used to me by now.

"Obedience, to the great head of the church." Devon started his speech, and I stuck my hands in my pocket. Toning him out, I was ready to piss all they ass off. I bet his ass won't force me to do shit else. When he grabbed my face to take me under, I held on to my wig with one hand, and sent the shit up with my other.

My ass went under that water, and the shit started bubbling. When they saw that shit, they ass started jumping out the water.

"What the hell?" Devon ass was cursing, and running at the same time.

"Don't curse now nigga. Who the fuck curses during a baptism anyway. Who raised your ass? I thought yall said sinners could be saved." My ass was in tears I was laughing so hard. They ass was running for the door. I guess they thought Lucifer himself was about to come out that mother fucker.

When I changed my clothes, and came outside. The nigga and everybody else had left me. Chuckling, I grabbed my phone and called Blaze. He lived the closest, and I was ready to get the fuck out of there. Plus, he was the only one of my kids that would find humor in this with my ass.

When he pulled up, I jumped in the car. His ass looked scared, and I almost forgot he burned my damn wigs up.

"Nigga quit acting like you about to get your ass beat. You owe me five thousand dollars for my wigs, and we even. Now, guess what I did." The nigga started laughing before I could even tell him.

"Ma, the entire world knows what you did. The shit gone viral on Facebook. They are talking about Armageddon is here. I damn near peed on myself. Why the fuck would you do that? That man got to be a damn fool if he still marries your ass." Laughing with him, I didn't want to let on that I was scared. Damn, what if I scared his ass off.

"You already got that man dealing with a wolf pussy, your mouth is bad, and now you done ran off the entire church. His ass probably half way to Mexico by now." His ass was joking, but I was having a panic attack.

What if I went too far this time? Wasn't no other nigga going to put up with my shit.

"I'll kill that nigga during Sunday School if he tried to leave me. You know it's only one way out of the Hoover Gang. We don't play that shit. If I need you, will you set him on fire for me?" Looking at me like I was crazy, his ass finally stopped laughing.

"It wasn't until this very moment that I realized you don't like my ass. Your bald-headed ass gone sit here and try to send me to hell. Get your ass out my car. I hope lightening strike on that velvet ass wig. You done lost your damn mind." Rolling my eyes at him, I got out his car. That nigga supposed to have my back. He was my special child. This nigga just put me out his car like a bitch had a fishy cat.

"Fuck you with your big back ass."

"I hope he left your ass." He laughed, but that shit scared the fuck out of me. Running in the house, his ass was in the front room pacing. Trying to play it cool, I acted as if I hadn't done shit.

"I'm about to cook some dinner. I hope you hungry. Your boo about to throw down in this mother fucker.

"Debra you have done a lot of things, but this was too far."

"What I do? Baby I been here all day." Maybe playing crazy would work.

"Debra, I took you to the church. I dipped your ass in the damn water, and you gone stand in my face and say you were here all day." I had fucked up, and it was only one thing I could do.

"You cheating on me? What bitch you had in your car? My ass been here all day trying on wigs. I told you I wasn't going to the church. I think you and Sister Thomas trying to pull one over on me. Now shut your ass up, and get ready to eat before you and that hoe piss me off." He pulled out his phone and started playing the video. Trying not to laugh, I had to bite the inside of my jaw. Their faces were priceless.

"Damn, that lady looks just like me. She gone have to leave the church though, it can only be one me in that mother fucker. You want some corn, or peas."

"Woman I'm not talking about no damn peas. Stop playing with me. You just embarrassed me and the church. Now if you want me to still marry you, your ass gone stop talking shit about being the first lady. You owe me, and I don't want to hear shit else about it." As long as he wasn't leaving, I would tell his ass anything he wanted to hear at this point.

"I still don't know what you are talking about, but I will be first lady. Now come dip in this tiger. She's growling."

"That's another thing, I'm not giving you no more until you go shave. A nigga tongue be caught up trying to find the spot I'm looking for. I want the tiger, but I ain't trying to go through the jungle to find her."

"Fuck you bitch, I know somebody like it." Walking off, I went to the kitchen to start dinner. When the water started boiling for the macaroni, I fell the fuck out laughing. Sometimes I was too much for my mother

fucking self.

REASON NUMBER 6

"She took me back, after I broke her heart about a thousand times. She gave her life to me, with no regrets she followed me. The girl she raised me, and I'm forever indebted to her cus. When a woman loves, she loves for real. When a woman loves she loves for real." When a woman loves- R. Kelly

ASH...

"Baby, can you get Zavia? My ass is tired, and I'm about to meet Juicy and them for a drink." From the look on his face, I knew some bullshit was coming.

"Ma, me and the brothers have a meeting. I'm already late, you gone have to take the kids with you. Yall ain't about to do shit but drink in the house and talk about us."

"I don't care if I was just sitting on the toilet. Baby I need a break. You know I can't enjoy myself with her. She is needy, and I need a night off. If you do this, I'll do that thing you like when you get home."

"How Sway? Your ass gone be drunk trying to do the lazy fuck. I'm not trying to be laying on my side like we in high school sneaking. If you want me to take them, you gone do the shit right now." When he folded his arms, I almost laughed at his ass. He was really trying to throw a tantrum.

"Go put her to sleep, I'm going to get ready for you big daddy." This nigga took off running and all I could do was laugh. He didn't mind taking Zavi with him, his ass was always trying to leave me with the baby. She was six months, but her ass was bad as hell. Her ass be all over the place, and gets into anything you put her by. Ass just be rolling.

Going into my closet, grabbed my Chinese bang wig, and put on my sexy gown. Getting the massage table, I set it up in the room. Making sure I had the right oils, I lit some candles, turned on some music, and waited for him to come in the room. As soon as he walked in and saw the setup, we jumped right into character.

"I have an appointment with Ming Lee for a massage. I'm a little early, but I have a meeting later."

"I Ming. Come come." Talking in my best Chinese accent, I led him to the table. "Take off clothes, and lay down." Doing as he was told, his ass got completely naked and laid on the table. Taking a sheet, I covered his mid-section. Grabbing my oils, I started massaging his back and shoulders. The music had the mood set right.

Working my way down to his legs, I bushed the tip of his dick every time I rubbed his inner thigh. His dick had to be hurting cus his ass was laying on top of it. Every time I brushed it, his dick jumped. Acting as if it was a mistake, I continued with his massage. Finishing his legs, I turned him over. Rubbing his arms and chest, had me turned all the way on.

"Ooh so strong. You muscles big." You could tell he was trying not to laugh.

"Something else is bigger." Ignoring him, I continued rubbing oil all over him. When I made it to his legs, I rubbed up against his dick. Standing straight up in the sheet, my mouth watered at the sight. "Do you mind if I take this off." Giving him the okay, he removed the sheet.

"Big black man. So big." Giving him a church pat on his dick, I kept massaging. Making my way back up, I started to slowly rub his balls. "Massage okay?" Nodding yes, he gave me the okay to keep going. "Happy ending extra. You have extra?" Nodding his head again, I poured some more oil in my hands.

His dick was so big, I had to use both hands to get a good rhythm going. His eyes closed from my touch, I knew he was about to bust and I increased the speed.

"How much for you to climb on this dick Ming? You wanna climb on this big black dick?"

"Lot of money. Black dick too big for Ming."

"Climb on the table, I'll help you." Putting my scared face on, I climbed on top. Pulling me to him, he sucked on my breast using his tongue to play with my nipples. While I was caught up in the motion of his tongue, he lifted my body to slide me down. Putting on a scared face, he guided me. Sliding inside of me, my body shuddered from his touch. His ass still had this effect on me.

"Ride this dick Ming. Daddy need you to ride this big black dick." Getting up on my feet, I went to work on that dick. You could hear his toes popping, but I wasn't stopping until he bust a nut. Spinning around on it, I rode him reverse cowboy and his ass started screaming out.

"Ooh shit Ming, spin around on it again. You riding the shit out of this dick." Sinning again to face him, I took off. That nigga was going crazy. Knowing he was not about to be long, I allowed my juices to flow. As soon as I was done shaking, his ass was cumming too. If I had wait any longer, I would have missed that train.

"Damn Ming, here go a stack. You earned every penny."

"You dick so big, me love you long time for two dollars." We both laughed and headed towards the shower. Knowing how he is, I washed my ass quick and got dressed. Running out to my car, I jumped in to take this ride to Juicy's house. My phone ringing brought me out of my thoughts of the bomb ass sex session me and my man just had. It was Drea.

"Hey boo, you left yet?"

"I just left out, I'm on the way."

"Can you stop by my house and tell Blaze to give you my wallet? I made a mistake and left it."

"Yea, but I'm taking all the money out of it."

"Girl, hurry your ass up. I've been here for an hour, and I'm drunk. Juicy keeps giving me two cups. Talking about I have to drink for you until you get here."

"I'll be there shortly. I'm headed to your house now." Laughing, I hung up the phone. I'm glad Juicy didn't hold any grudges against Drea. She better than me, I don't know if I could be cool with someone that fucked my nigga. The way Blaze is over Drea, I'm sure she fucked his ass good too.

When I pulled up to Blaze's house, I didn't get out of the car. I was stuck watching this lady walk inside with him. He hugged her at the door, and then shut that mother fucker. Bitch was bad as hell too. Now the shit Kimmie was saying was coming back to bite us in the ass. Pulling my phone out, I called Drea back.

"Hey bitch, I'm at your house and Blaze just went inside with a woman. A thick ass pretty bitch too. They hugged and went inside. Get your ass here now."

"On the way. The bitch better pray to the Gods her ass is gone before I get there. It's about to go DOWN."

"Hurry up. I'm gone stay in the car and watch until you get here. I don't want him to know you on the way." Looking at the phone, I realized her ass had hung up and was on the way.

My nerves were shot, and now my mind was fucking with me. Was Quick ass out here cheating too. They did everything together, there was no way he was the only one being faithful. Baby Face already cheated, Shadow ass is cheating, and now Blaze. Quick ass better be happy with Ming Lee, I'll kill the shit out of that nigga.

They ass got us fucked up, and I was sick of niggas thinking they can do what they want. Easing out of my car, I grabbed my bat out of the trunk. Blaze wasn't my

man, but I was about to beat his ass like he was. As soon

as Drea got her ass here, we were about to put in work.

QUICK...

I don't know how anybody could ever cheat on

they bitch once they found the one. Ash ass be putting

in work, and she had my ass gone like a mother fucker.

That pussy was A1 and I couldn't wait to get some of

that drunk shit. Her ass get real nasty when she drunk. I

don't even think she remember half the shit I have her

doing on them drunk nights.

One night I came all in her ear. The next day her

ass kept complaining about not being able to hear. My

ass just laughed and acted like I ain't know what the fuck was going on. Just thinking about that as I packed up the baby bag had my ass in tears. Grabbing the kids, I headed out of the door. The meeting was at Blaze's house today, because the planner needed to see the layout of his house. We were turning it into a night on the island. Mama didn't want to watch the kids while we go on vacation.

Her ass said it's her day too. Not wanting to leave the kids with a baby sitter for that long, we decided to bring the island to them. Sand and all. The shit was going to be dope as hell, and I couldn't wait to see what she had planned. My girl deserves it all, and I plan to give it to her. When I pulled up, I saw the girls standing in the street, and I didn't know what the fuck was going on.

Trying to see if they knew what we were up to, I let my window down to try and hear them. They ass was so into it, they didn't even realize I pulled up.

"Naw fuck busting some windows, I got a trick for his ass." I had no idea what or who Drea was talking about. She took off towards the back of the house, and the other girls stood there talking. When I saw Drea round that corner pouring gasoline, I jumped out of the car. I didn't want to leave the baby, but I had to stop her. I didn't make it to the gate. Ash ass hit me with a bat.

"What the fuck. Have you lost your mind?" She looked like a wild woman.

"Fuck yeah, and you about to lose your legs and your dick. Issa cripple." Her ass started swinging that bat, and all I could do was crawl my ass back to the car.

Jumping in, I knew that was the only way she would

stop.

"You gone bust the windows with your kids in

here?" Looking pissed, she walked off towards Blaze

Truck. Grabbing my phone, I saw the flames and knew

Drea had set the house on fire. These mother fuckers

were on some other shit. This nigga answered all happy

not knowing his ass was about to be French toast.

"Nigga, your girl set the house on fire. Get your

ass out of there."

"Fuck you talking about? Drea at Juicy house."

This nigga wants explanations and shit.

"Nigga, I'm sitting outside. Your girl just set your

house on fire, Ash just beat me with a bat, and now they

are tearing your truck up. Once they done with that, you

know the Phantom next. Get the fuck out here."

Hanging up the phone, I could see him and the woman

running out of the house. Getting back out of the car, I

had to help him. They were fucking Blaze ass up with

them bats. The planner tried to run away, and Juicy

upper cut her ass. We were about to be paying a hefty

settlement behind they bullshit.

"Hey nigga what the fuck is going on? What the

hell Blaze do now?" Baby Face had finally arrived.

"I have no idea. They done lost their minds. Ash

just beat me with a bat, now they are attacking him. As

you can see Drea set the house on fire. With the nigga in

it." Running towards the girls, we approached them

cautiously.

"Ladies, listen. I don't know what's wrong, but it's not what it looks like."

"How you know what the fuck it looks like? You just brought your egg yolk looking ass over here. Don't worry, you're next." Drea had to be drunk, she never talked like this.

"She is an event planner. We were planning Valentine's Day. Where the fuck would you get an idea like that from?" They looked at each other breathing hard as hell. The event planner jumped up, and ran like her ass was in the fucking Olympics.

"Oh, my bad. Carry on. Come on girls." This mother fucking Ash thought shit was sweet.

"Fuck that, I'm getting my licks back. You beat me like a field nigga." Blaze grabbed Drea, and pinned her down on the ground.

"Valentine's Day is cancelled. Your ass ain't getting shit but a heart." This nigga pulled out his lighter and burned a heart on Drea's chest. "Crazy ass mother fucker. Look at our house. You lucky my mama got the kids. Your ass didn't even know they weren't in there. Look at my fucking truck. Man, Quick give me my fucking money right now. Or I'm burning my name on your girl ass." Now they ass was standing there looking stupid.

"We're sorry. I thought. I saw the woman, and the shit Kimmie was saying. I'm sorry." Ash tried using tears.

"Fuck a sorry. Look at my mother fucking knee. You ugly mother fuckers got my shit looking like I got gout." Blaze was mad as hell.

"Bro, you can't get gout in the knee." Baby Face already knew not to say shit.

"Nigga I said it's gout. Imma be walking down the aisle and they ass gone be laughing. Look at gout knee Blaze." Grabbing my phone, I guess I had to be the only one with sense and call the fire department. "I hope they lock your ass up. Cus I'm telling. Yup, that snitching ass nigga Blaze with the gout knee." We laughed as his ass he limped off. Drea looked scared, but we knew he wasn't gone turn her in. His knee was fucked up though.

"Yall fucked up big this time. Ash take my car, and go the fuck home. We have to clean up the mess yall insecure asses made. Just remember, now he has to stay

with one of us. Somebody gone be getting fucked up."

Everybody looked scared, but it was the fucking truth. I

prayed that nigga didn't come to my house.

JUICY...

Today was Valentine's Day and me and the girls

were looking bout dumb as fuck. We read that shit all

wrong, and there was nobody to blame but Ash. Fuck

yeah, I said it. Her ass called us saying she saw Blaze with

a bitch, everybody knows how we coming. Now here it

is, couple's day, and we are drinking looking at each

other with the dumb grin.

"Ash you know this is all your fault right. You should have gotten better intel before you called Drea." Everybody nodded their head in agreeance with me.

"Bitch you tried it. Didn't nobody tell Drea ass to go all Angela Bassett from waiting to exhale. We could have kicked the door in and saw that the bitch was an event planner. Instead, she done torched they shit, and now her crazy ass nigga living in our shit." Ash was mad, but she still laughed.

"Nope, not my fault. But since we are blaming bitches, may as well start with Kimmie. If her ass never put the seed in our heads, we wouldn't have thought shit was going on. Only nigga out here cheating is crooked dick."

"To the left, to the left. To the right, to the right."

We all laughed at Drea as we sung the electric slide. That

nigga be curving that dick in some bitches.

"Fuck yall. I thought yall was confident and shit.

Sounds to me like yall know it was some truth in what I

was saying." Kimmie was still on that bullshit, but I

wasn't going for it today.

"You can try that shit if you want to, but not only

are you getting out of my shit, but you are going with a

well whooped ass. Now pass me some wings, your ass

think you gone talk shit and eat up all the food. Bitch

please." Everybody laughed, but that shit ended quick

when we heard the front door open. The kids were with

the guys, so we had no idea who was walking in our shit.

From past experiences, anything could happen. Each of

us grabbing our gun, we waited to see who was

rounding the corner. Our nerves were shot, until each of

the guys rounded the corner with a single rose.

"Now yall gone shoot us? Put that shit up before

you cheddar bob yourselves." Not wanting to shoot

myself in the pussy, I put my gun up and ran to my man.

"Even though you fucked up, we still love yall ugly

asses. Now let's go." When Quick started talking, Ash

ran to her man as well. As we got ready to walk out, a

sadness came over Kimmie that broke my heart. Out of

nowhere, Shadow rounded the corner with a rose.

Everyone had tears in their eyes, and was happy for her.

You could tell she wanted to play upset, but even she

couldn't deny the love that was in the room. Following

our men hand and hand, we let them lead us to a night

of love.

When we pulled up to the main house, you could

tell all the women was saying what the fuck in our

heads. What in the fuck was special about Valentine's at

the main house? Damn near breaking my ankle I was

stomping so hard, we went inside. I wanted to slap the

shit out of Face. Knowing they only did this shit because

we fucked up, made me want to take my tear back for

Kimmie. It was all her fault, and I wish I could take my

wings back too.

When the lights came on, I was glad I held my

tongue. It was beautiful inside. Sand was everywhere,

and they started to remove their shoes. Following suit, it

was the first time I was speechless. These niggas had a

horse in the house, a bar made up, cabanas, hammocks,

the works. It was as if we were on vacation on one of the

islands. Me and the girl's looked at each other, and

everyone was teary eyed. This shit was special as fuck,

and I couldn't wait to give my man some. He deserved

some pussy after this shit.

"You want to go horse back riding with me baby?"

Not wanting to piss the horse off riding his ass inside the

house, I decided to pass. Nigga fuck around and buck,

might toss my ass down the stairs.

"No thank you baby." Grabbing my hand, he

pulled me to him.

"Let's dance." Grabbing me by ass, my man slid his

tongue in my mouth. How in the fuck were we supposed

to dance with no music?

"Baby how." Before I could finish my question, a live band appeared and started to play music. As tears filled my eyes, I allowed my man to lead me through the sand. Everyone else started doing the same, and it was the best gift I had ever been given. This man was a blessing from God with a big dick. Nothing could be better than this.

BLAZE...

Today was the day of my mama's wedding, and I knew it was about to be a damn circus act. People say I'm aggy, but my mama was worse than all of us. That wig toting shit drop does the most at times, and I know that's who I get that shit from. Speaking of petty, I was

on my way to do some bullshit as we speak. Easing into

Spark's room, I woke her up.

"Hey baby, I need you to do something for daddy.

You want to help daddy?"

"Yes, Spark help daddy." Kissing her, I passed her

a lighter. That nigga Quick thought he had gotten away

with that slick shit he said. Not wanting everybody

cursing me out on my mother's wedding, I'm using my

daughter to do my dirty work.

"Uncle Quick wants to play fire race. You have to

set him on fire first, or you lose. You want to win baby

girl?" When she nodded her head yes, I knew she was

going to do what I asked. Not that I had to force her to

play with fire, I just needed her to make sure she lit the

right shit on fire. Her ass will burn down the whole house without guidance. Putting her on the floor, I let her run to Quick's room. He wouldn't stay mad at her if she did it. Laughing at my own bullshit, I went in my room to wake Drea up.

"Get up girl, you know it takes you longer to wash that ass. You got extra pussy lips and shit." My baby laughed, and that's what I loved most about her. Anybody else would feel I needed to let it go. The fact that we were still together showed that I forgave her. I just like to talk shit. That loose ass pussy was good as fuck, and she had a nigga gone.

"Shut up, if your dick wasn't so little, maybe it wouldn't feel loose. Now move the fuck out of the way so I can go shower."

"Your ass better get those lips." Laughing, she smacked me when we heard Quick screaming. "What the fuck?" Running out of the room, we headed to see what all the commotion was.

"After the wedding, yall getting the fuck out of my house. You and the devil's spawn gotta get up out of here." Trying to look appalled, I put on my most concerned face.

"What happened? Spark, what did you do." Jumping in my arms, she told me what happened.

"Me played fire race like you told me. I beat Uncle Quick." Dropping her ass to the floor, I couldn't believe her snitch ass told.

"I ain't tell her shit bro. Let me see, how bad is it." When that nigga turned around, I knew he was putting my ass out. I couldn't stop laughing at the George

Jefferson patch on the side of his head. She burned all

his hair off on the right side. I legit had tears in my eyes.

"You think this shit funny? I should shoot the shit

out of your ass." Flicking my Bic, he turned and walked

off. Heading back to the room, I kicked her and kept it

moving. My ass might not be the daddy, cus no child of

mine would have told that fast. Everyone started getting

ready for the wedding, as I laughed my ass off.

****

Me, Quick, and Shadow stood up front as we

waited on our mom to walk down the aisle. Everybody

thought me, and Shadow were crying from happiness,

but the truth was, we couldn't stop laughing at that

nigga head. Trying my best to look out towards the

crowd, I noticed that Suave, and Gangsta came with their girls. Giving them a nod, the music began to play, and it was time. After R. Kelly tried to kiss my bitch on our wedding, I refused to let his ass sing today. Kenny Latimore's For You played as Spark came down the aisle throwing flowers. My baby looked beautiful, and Zavi was right behind her carrying the rings.

When our wives came down the aisle, the shit took me back to our wedding day. I would marry my wife ten more times. She was the baddest bitch in the world to me, and she got me. Baby Face appeared with my mama on his arm, and I ain't gone lie, the shit brought a tear to my eye. All we had were each other, and that's all the fuck we needed. The fucking Hoover

Gang, a nigga was damn near about to shed a tear until I heard my mama's voice.

"Why didn't nobody tell me these fine ass niggas was gone be here? I would have worn my other wig. Before I go up there and say I do, let me know now if I can get a shot of some that good good." Everyone gasped, and I just knew Paradise was about to beat my mama's ass. When Gangsta shook his head no, her face twisted up.

"Nigga I wasn't talking to you. Didn't I tell your ass you wasn't about to kill my tiger? Sit your psycho ass down, if I need to kill Devon, then I'll call you. I'm talking to Suave." Knowing this was about to get out of hand, Face tried to drag my mama towards the front.

"Do you realize you just told the church you were premeditating murder? Get your simple ass up there and say I do before your man change his mind. Don't make no sense how the fuck you act." You could tell Face pissed her off.

"Don't be cursing in the damn church, who raised your ass? And stop pulling me like that, you got my damn wig twisting." Fixing her hair, she started down the aisle again. Quick shook his head, and I laughed my ass off. "Fuck you shaking your head for? Up here looking like project grass. Move." Pushing Quick back, she had the nerve to stand in front of Devon and smile. That nigga needed to run for the hills. Not wanting my mama to look a mess on her wedding day, I tried to help her out.

"Ma, fix your wig. That shit look post mortem. Turn it to the left or something. Fluff that bitch up." I tried to whisper it, but you know my mama ain't got no sense.

"Nigga you saying I'm dead?" Her ass was offended.

"Naw, but that wig is bruh."

"Blaze I'll beat your ass. Don't front me nigga." Some lady stood up, and you could tell shit was about to go all bad.

"Ms. Hoover, you are in a church. This is ridiculous. Reverend Sims, you need to say something. This is who you want our first lady to be, someone who don't even know how to talk in a church."

"Bitch it ain't shit but a building. We can turn this mother fucker into a boxing ring. You got me twisted." Mama was going off, but I needed to correct her.

"No ma, your wig is though. For real, fix that shit." Pushing me out of the way, she turned to Devon.

"Baby, go get me some water. Sons, you know what to do. Five minutes." When she tried to go down the steps, we all stopped her. There was no way we were letting her fight on her wedding day.

"Ma, look at that man. He is standing there with a bottle of water like you asked. That man loves you, anybody else would have left your ass. Now get up there and say I do before he changes his mind. Fixing her dress, she headed back to her spot. Making sure her wig was straight, I decided not to say a word. All hell just broke loose, and I wasn't about to kick that shit back off.

The pastor officiating took them through their vows.

Once he told Devon to kiss his bride, I was glad we made

it through.

"Don't get in my face like that, I'll bite your nose

clean off. Fuck is you doing?" This lady just couldn't stop

acting up.

"Baby, he said kiss your bride, that's all I was

doing." Devon looked stressed the hell out.

"That's what you better be doing. You can kiss

something else later after we get rid of all these niggas."

Laughing, we walked down the aisle with our mother.

You never knew what you would get with a Hoover. That

was who the fuck we were.

CREEPING WITH MY

VALENTINE

REASON NUMBER SEVEN

"On the perfect day, I know that I can count on you. When that's not possible, tell me can you weather the storm. Cus I need somebody who will stand by me. Through the good times, and bad times she will always. Always be right there. Sunny days, everybody loves them tell me baby can you stand the rain." Can you stand the rain- New Edition

RENEGADE...

I done did a lot of shit in the streets, but getting ready to be a father was one of the hardest things a nigga had to do. Lai wasn't shit like Megan when she was pregnant. This girl was mean as hell and I couldn't

wait for the baby to come. The entire pregnancy, I was

already scared as shit that something would happen to

the baby because of the last situation. That's some shit I

couldn't take again, and Lai made sure this shit wasn't

easy on a nigga.

She did everything the doctors told her not to. The

late-night store runs were really driving a nigga crazy.

I've never seen no shit like this, and Megan was extra as

fuck. Her ass wanted shit at three in the morning that I

couldn't see someone eating if they ass was hungry.

Right now, my ass was on a store run. Tonight, it was

peanut butter, jelly, and tuna.

Knowing there wasn't a store on earth that made

that shit, I had to make a few stops in order to get it.

Looking down at my ringing phone, Shay was calling me again for the umpteenth time. I haven't talked to her ass since I fucked her in the shop while Megan listened, and I didn't plan on talking to her now. All I needed from her was a meeting with me and her father. A nigga been got that, and business was booming.

Lai was driving me crazy, but I was happy as fuck. There was no way I was letting her ass come between us like she did with me and Megan. Shay was the straw that broke the camel's back in me and her relationship. It was what led me to Laila in the first place, and there was no other place I would rather be.

As soon as I pulled up to the house, my phone started to ring again. Seeing that it was Shay, I powered my phone off and walked in the crib. I left her ass in

Houston, and that's how I planned to keep it. Lai was sitting on the couch sleeping, and I swear she looked sexy as fuck. If it wasn't for her big ass belly, you wouldn't even know she was pregnant. Everything about her turned me on.

"Baby, wake up. Here, I got your food. Lai wake your ass up and get this shit." Her mouth was hanging open, and I was tempted to put my dick in her shit. I wasn't fucking with her ass though. A nigga learned his lesson the last time. She went to bed hungry, and woke up chewing on my shit. Dick looked like beef jerky for two weeks.

"What you get me? I had to go to sleep, or I was gone die from starvation. Took your ass forever to bring me my stuff. Slow ass nigga."

"Lai, I was gone twenty minutes, and I had to go all over the city to find that shit. How the fuck was I gone find that shit in one store." Her mean ass snatched the bag from me, and took the sandwich out. Watching her ass take one bite, she sat it down and closed her eyes again.

"You had me go all over the fucking city for one bite? Your ass better eat that shit." Rolling her eyes at me, she put the shit in the refrigerator.

"I'm full, I'll eat it tomorrow." Me and her both knew that was a lie. We had a fridge full of shit that she never touches again. Her ass be having me rushing home, and then don't eat the shit. Walking over to the freezer, she grabbed a popsicle. The way she sucked it, got my dick hard as fuck. No longer mad, I was determined to get some pussy. Walking up behind her, I ran my fingers up her pussy.

"Baby, gone now. I'm not in the mood. I'm tired, and I need to go to sleep. You know I get sleepy after I eat."

"Spread your fucking legs." You could tell she was trying to fight it, but her pussy was going against her. Grabbing her by her neck, I was done playing with her ass. "Spread your fucking legs Lai."

As is if she had no say so over her body, her legs opened. Pushing her over the counter the best way I could, I kept one hand on her neck, and pushed her pajama shorts over to the side. I was gone play with that pussy until it got wet, but it was already soaking.

Pulling my dick out, I slid it inside her. A nigga been trying to take my time with her since she was so close to delivery, but tonight, I was about to beat that shit up. They say Valentine's Day is for women, and this pussy was gone be my gift. Her ass was due on the seventeenth, and I knew it was gone be a while before I get some pussy.

Her ass been turning me down, but I was over that shit. I had two weeks to dig in these guts, and I was gone get this shit.

"Why the fuck you holding your moan in? The neighbors better hear you. The longer you fight it, the worse it's going to be." She tried to give me a baby ass moan, and she was about to learn today. Tightening my grip around her neck, I pushed my dick in hard and fast. I was aiming for her cervix, and she knew it. Screaming as

loud as she could, her ass finally complied.

"Fuck baby, yes. Fuck this pussy." You know, that's

exactly what the fuck I did. Once her body started

shaking, I tightened up on her neck speeding up my

pumps. Fuck, my nut came out so strong, my dick

wouldn't stop jerking.

"Go upstairs and get in the shower, I'll be up there

for round two."

SHAY...

This nigga Renegade had me fucked up if he

thought he could ignore me. I'm the reason his ass was

the king of the Chi. Now he wanna treat me like I was a

hoe on the streets. My daddy was his connect, but I planned to change all of that since he wanted to play me. Taking a flight to the DR, I stormed into my father's office.

"Hello to you too daughter." You could tell he was annoyed with me just popping up, but I didn't give a fuck. "Where is my grandson?"

"With the nanny. That's why I'm here. You can no longer supply Renegade. That nigga thinks he can ignore me, and we have a child together." This nigga was trying to hold his laughter in, but the amusement showed all over his face.

"You want me to fuck up my money over some lover's quarrel bullshit? You don't even know if he is the father, but you're labeling him a deadbeat. Shay, I raised you better than this. The man didn't even know you were pregnant, let alone had the baby. Quit whining, and do what you need to do as a mother. You created this mess, you clean it up." This nigga was pissed like he was getting shitted on.

"I don't care what he doesn't know. I've been calling him, and he won't even answer for us to get this situated. At the end of the day, I'm your daughter. I said I want him cut off, and that's that." Getting up from behind his desk, he walked over to me.

"Get your spoiled ass the fuck out of my house before I forget you're my daughter. You come in here demanding shit like you don't know who the fuck I am. That man makes me more money than any of my distributors. The fuck I look like cutting him off because you don't know who you fucked. Go home, before I

embarrass your ass. You created it, clean it up." When

he walked out, I knew he was dismissing me. My ass

done came all the way over here for nothing, but I

wasn't done. He had me fucked up, and I was

determined to make his ass hear me.

****

As soon as I got back to Houston, I got my baby

ready and headed back to the plane. Giving him one

more chance to answer, I called his phone. Sending me

to voicemail each time, I was over his bullshit. Using my

connections, I had my people get me his address.

The entire flight, I thought about what could

happen once I showed up at his door. He is a ruthless

killer, and I know it could go wrong for me. However; I

was willing to take that chance. I'm Shay, and this nigga was treating me like Sheba the alley cat.

Getting off the plane, my nerves were shot to shit. I wasn't scared to tell him about the baby, but that nigga was a loose cannon when he wanted to be. Even though my father talked shit, if Renegade did anything to me, he wouldn't live to see the next day. I was still his child, and no one would fuck with the connects daughter.

Pulling into his driveway, I made sure the baby was wrapped up good, and got out. Chicago had a different type of cold, and I didn't need my baby getting sick. Throwing all fucks to the wind, I rang the doorbell. As soon as the door swung open, I knew this shit wasn't about to go well. This big belly bitch was standing there looking at me like she was ready to fight, and my ass was standing there with this baby looking like I was losing

Isaiah. May as well get the shit over with.

"Hi, is Renegade here?" She turned her face up,

and I knew being nice was not gone last long.

"Bitch you better turn your ass around and go the

fuck back where you came from. This ain't that, and I

don't mind beating a bitch to sleep today." She was a

feisty one, and I wouldn't mind having her pussy in my

mouth.

"Bitch please. Get Renegade before your man be

broke starving and gang banging. If he still wants his

connect, he better bring his ass to the door." Yeah I lied,

but so what. She didn't need to know my daddy wasn't

gone stop his flow.

"Oh, let me show you where I lost the fucks I could give. Bitch I don't give a fuck about no connect. You got five seconds to drag your big foot ass off my porch, or shit about to go wrong for you." Before I could check this hoe, Renegade showed up.

"Baby who at the door? Shay what the fuck." His eyes trailed down to the baby, and I could tell his mind was putting it together.

"I came to bring you your son. If you had answered your phone, you would know what the fuck I was doing here." The girl never gave him a reason to explain, she slapped his ass so hard spit flew from his mouth.

"Lai, don't get fucked up. I don't know what she talking about, so don't start that shit." Their exchange was amusing, but I wasn't here for that.

"When yall done fighting, I still need to know what you gone do. I ain't got all day." The girl walked up to me, and I thought she was about to hit me while I had my son in my arms. Snatching back the covers, she looked at him.

"Ain't no way that's Renegade baby. Ugly ass lil boy. Girl gone back home and call the real daddy. Look like he is leading me through the tunnels. Follow me I know zee way." Laughing at her own joke, she walked off unbothered.

"Look I'm not trying to start no shit, but you wouldn't answer. You need to step up and be a father, or you gone be a broke deadbeat. You know my father

ain't gone go for the bullshit."

"If you were so concerned with me being a daddy,

why am I just now hearing about a baby? Why the fuck

you ain't reach out when you found out you were

pregnant? You on some bullshit, and I'm not with it."

"Nigga please, you act like you a prize or some

shit. Your bitch was a better lay than you, and this one

look like she might be even better." That nigga was

pissed, and I knew he would try to kill me if I fucked this

one.

"Try it if you want to. You won't live to blink twice.

Meet me at the hospital tomorrow, and we will take a

DNA. Until we get the results, stay the fuck away from

me.

Slamming the door in my face, he didn't even look

at the baby. It's all good though, once we took the test,

he wouldn't have a choice. Yeah, I was sleeping with a

couple of niggas, but the time frame match up with my

one night stand with Renegade. His ass wasn't gone

have a choice but to come around once those test

results came back.

LAILA...

This nigga and this raggedy ass bitch got me

fucked up. I waddled my ass away from the door like I

was unbothered, but I was hurt. He never told me

anything about this bitch, and now I doubted everything

he told me. Was he still sleeping with her? Did he know

she was pregnant? Would he want her now? A million questions flooded my mind as I put on my shoes and grabbed my purse. I had to get the fuck out of here before I hurt his ass. I been through too much with Niko, a bitch wasn't going through this again.

"Lai, where the fuck are you going?" He was trying to mask his anger, but I didn't give a fuck how he felt.

"Out of here. I thought you and your baby mama wanted to spend some time with the gremlin." Walking past him, I headed down the stairs.

"Lai don't play with me. We are going to talk about this, and your ass gone let me explain."

"Explain what? You killed my nigga, so you could do me worse than he did me. Save the bullshit, and get the fuck out of my face." Renegade closed the space, and I wanted to suck the shit out of his lips. He was sexy

as fuck, but I needed to stay mad. My hormones kicked

in at the wrong times.

"You killed my bitch, now what. Don't play that

shit with me Lai. You know what it is, and you know

damn well I ain't know shit about a baby. We taking a

DNA tomorrow, and we will cross that bridge when we

get there."

"I'm not crossing shit but the street, when I leave

your ass. I'm not raising another woman's baby. You

may as well call her back, and see where yall can go with

it." Of course, I didn't mean that, but I needed him to

hurt like I was hurting.

"What about Valentine's Day. All the plans I had

for us, and what about when you go into labor? Fuck

that too?" Laughing like a maniac, I couldn't believe he was sitting here talking about a damn Valentine's Day.

"Nigga fuck you and that day. I might call you when I go in labor. Get the fuck out of my face." Pushing past him, I walked out of the door. As soon as I got in my car, the tears fell. Everything was going perfect, and now this. The way he has been acting, I thought he was gone propose on Valentine's Day, not bring home a baby.

Knowing the first place he would look was Jada's, or Jazzy's, I headed downtown to a hotel. All I wanted to do was eat, cry, and listen to I hate you songs. Tomorrow, I would think about everything that was going on, and what the situation was. Tonight, I just wanted to hate him. In my heart, I know Renegade wouldn't do anything to hurt me, but the shit didn't hurt any less. I meant what I said though. I've accepted a lot

of things, but an outside baby wasn't one. I wasn't built

for that kind of shit, and quite frankly, I didn't want to.

When I checked into the hotel, I made sure I used

his card. This Trump bill was on his ass. The first thing I

did was call room service, and ordered any and

everything I could think of. As soon as I laid across the

bed, my phone rung. Seeing it was Jada, I answered.

"What's up bitch." Trying to act as if nothing was

wrong, I talked like I normally do.

"You tried it. Your man just left from over here.

His ass is out there on a rampage looking for you. Where

the fuck are you, and why didn't you call me?"

"That's why. I knew yall would be the first place

he would look. I'm good though. My ass just need a

moment to think." You could hear her moving around,

and then she came back on the line.

"Fuck that, tell me where you are, and I'm on the

way. Quan's ass can keep the baby, I need a girl's night.

You need a shoulder, and we need some drinks. Well, I

do you can have cranberry juice."

"I'm at the Trump. Room 1342. If Renegade show

up at my door, I promise I'm done talking to you."

"Fuck him, I'm on the way." Laying down, I waited

on Jada and room service to come. Turning the Tv on,

every damn commercial was about Valentine's Day. I

turned that shit right back off. Closing my eyes, I figured

I could rest until they came.

My ass must have dozed off longer than I thought, the knocking on the door woke me up. Seeing it was Jada, I let her in.

"Now what happened. You know that nigga left a bunch of shit out. I need the tea bitch." This hoe ain't shit, she ain't come over here to help me.

"Your ass only came to be nosy. I should put your ass out without telling you a mother fucking thing." Room service interrupted us, and I let them in. After we had all the food, I decided to tell her what went down.

"So, thiis bitch knocked on my door like she was the po- po, and had the nerve to ask for him. Said the baby his. Girl that baby is fifty shades of naw Sway. I told her the ugly ass baby ain't his, and walked off. His ass tried to talk, but I left. That's it." Her mouth was open.

"Babies are not ugly, why would you tell that girl that? What did Renegade say about you calling his son ugly?" Now the bitch was throwing shade.

"Imma let you make it, but don't push me too far. He said they gone test it, but I didn't stick around to hear anything else." The hoe rolled her eyes, and I was ready to put her out.

"Girl, you could have at least heard him out. He is not Niko and you have to remember that shit. I know his dirty dick ass hurt you, but you have a good man. You need to find out what the fuck happened. Plus, bitch you fucking up Valentine's Day. His ass gone fuck around and get you one of them monkeys." We both laughed, but mine was fake as fuck. It was so much on my mind. I wasn't trying to lose my man, but I wasn't trying to get played again either. No matter how much you think a

nigga is the one, they will find a way to fuck that shit up.

The devil on my shoulder keeps whispering how he

cheated on his bitch with me. Looking at Jada brought

me out of my trans.

"Bitch if you don't get your feet off my bed. I

thought Quan was making you get your feet done now.

Them bitches is scratching. You too old for that shit."

Scraping her feet all over my bed, she got real

comfortable in my shit.

"First off, this ain't your bed. It belongs to the

orange one. Second, I just got my feet done two days

ago. Third, you need to be worried about who feet your

man about to be lying next to since your ass around here

leaving niggas." The only thing I heard was she just got them feet done.

"How Sway? You need to see a doctor if they back looking like that days later. Now get the fuck out, I'm sleepy. I'll talk to Renegade tomorrow." Getting off the bed, she put her boots back on, and headed towards the door.

"Bye bitch." I hope his ass was willing to talk tomorrow. Laying down, that was the last thing on my mind.

RENEGADE...

How the fuck could this be my life right now. I couldn't believe Shay ass showing up with baby Alf. If shorty was mine, imma keep a hat and blanket throwed

over his ass. Lil nigga was an awwww, waiting to

happen. That lil boy look like he had it rough in wild life.

Thinking I knew my girl, I grabbed my keys and headed

to Quan's house. She only fucked with Jada, and Jazzy.

She had to be at one of they shit.

        When I pulled up, I didn't see her car, but I was

about to interrogate the fuck out of Jada. Ringing the

bell, Quan let me in.

        "Fuck wrong with you nigga?" Quan always knew

when something was wrong with me. The shit was gone

come out eventually, so I went on and told him. Jada

walked in the room right as I sat down.

        "You talked to Lai?" When she shook her head no,

I could tell she wasn't lying. "Bruh, why Shay show up at

my house with a lil boy saying it's my son. Lai went the

fuck off and left, not giving me a chance to explain shit.

If she ain't come here, maybe she with Jazzy."

"Naw, she would come here first. Ain't no telling

where her ass at. You fucked up. Niko ain't even have a

baby on her, you done topped his ass." Trying not to

knock my homie's girl out, I ignored her comment.

"Jada take your ass on somewhere. He ain't even

talking to your thick heel ass. Go use that pedi egg I

bought you. Bruh, I just got her feet done two days ago.

Look at this shit. It's so much white shit on her feet, the

shit falling off. How the fuck you got dandruff on your

feet?" Stomping away, she went upstairs.

"Bruh, imma get out of here. Me and Shay going to take a DNA test tomorrow. This bitch got me fucked up. The baby ugly as shit too. Ain't no way his ass mine."

"You dumb as hell. I hope he ain't yours bruh. Lai ain't gone take care of somebody else ugly ass baby. I'll holla at you tomorrow. Go find your girl." When I left out, I headed back home hoping Lai brought her ass back to the house. A nigga was stressing, and I ain't even did shit. Jumping in the shower, I needed to clear my mind. When I got out, my phone was ringing. Looking at the name, I saw it was Quan.

"What's up bro."

"Nigga I been calling your ass. I know where your girl at. I walked in on her and Jada talking. You know she always talk on speaker phone. She at the Trump room

1342. Jada on her way there now, so give it a little time before you show your ass up."

"Aight bet. Good looking out." Hitting end, I got dressed, grabbed her some clothes, and headed out. Stopping at the store, I grabbed all the weird shit I could think of that she been wanting. I know she wasn't gone leave out and go get her own shit, so I was gone take it to her. After grabbing everything I thought she may need, I drove downtown. Texting Quan, I made sure Jada was gone before I went up.

Once he gave me the okay, I stopped at the front desk. The bitch was so busy flirting with me, I ain't even have to pay her to give me a room key. Her ass was willing to do anything I asked just to smile in my face.

Walking in the room, all the lights were off. Only the light from outside shined inside. Putting everything down, I walked over to her. Even though she looked peaceful, I could tell she was hurt. Dried tears were all down her face, and that shit broke a nigga's heart. Leaning down, I kissed her. A moan escaped her mouth, but she continued to lightly snore. Taking my clothes off, I climbed in bed with her. Pulling her close to me, I wanted her to know I was right here when she woke up.

****

My face felt like it was burning, as I remembered where I was. Opening my eyes, Lai slapped the shit out of me again. She had a peppermint inside of a pickle eating it, looking at me with death in her eyes.

"How the fuck you gone sit there and eat the shit I brought, but fight me for being here? We need to talk, well I do. You can listen. Megan cheated on me with Shay, and I fucked her while Megan listened to get back at her. I've never had a thing with her, and don't want her. I haven't even talked to her ass once she gave over the connect. She was blowing me up, and I wouldn't answer. I have no idea how she got the address. Her daddy is the plug, so I'm sure it wasn't hard for her."

"It was before my time, but it don't hurt any less. I won't be the first one to give you a baby, and I'm not playing step mama to that ugly ass lil boy. Mother fuckers gone be thinking that's my baby." Laughing, I grabbed her to me.

"Let's cross that bridge when we get there. We gone take the test today, and from there we will see what it is. I'm not letting you go because I haven't done shit." Leaning down, she kissed me with the juices from the nasty ass shit she was eating. "We good."

"Yea we good."

"Well come suck this dick then."

"Nigga you tried it, let's go get this test done." Dragging, I got dressed and called Shay phone.

"Meet me at UIC in fifteen minutes." Hanging up, me and Lai left out. Noticing she didn't get in the car with me, told me she may get pissed again and leave. Hoping this shit went right, I went to the hospital. Parking, I walked to the front of the building to wait for

Lai. She always drove slow, so I knew she was behind

me. Who didn't expect to see standing there was Quan.

"Nigga what the fuck are you doing here?" His ass

shrugged, and laughed.

"I had to see this uglass baby. No way I was letting

this shit pass me by. Is that him?" Looking over, it was an

old ass mind walking up. I hated this nigga with my soul

sometimes.

"Shut the fuck up." Lai finally waddled her ass up,

and right after was Shay. As soon as I saw her, I wanted

to knock her ass out. She walked up and tried to hand

me the baby. Swerving her ass, I went and held Lai's

hand. Quan walked up, and pulled the blanket down to

see the baby.

"Awww issa puppy." Shay snatched the baby back as the rest of us laughed. This nigga ain't got no sense, and I prayed the baby wouldn't be mine. Quan would never let me live that shit down.

"Let's get this shit over with." Heading inside, I got swabbed for some shit that could make or break my relationship. I was gone have to go way out for Valentine's Day to fix this shit.

REASON NUMBER EIGHT

"Some people live for the fortune. Some people live just for the fame. Some live for the power. Some people live just to play the game. Some people think that the physical things define what's within, and I been here before. That life's a bore. So full of the superficial. Some people want it all, but I don't want nothing at all, if it ain't you baby." If I ain't got you- Alicia Keys

QUAN...

This shit with Renegade had my ass stressing, and it wasn't even my mess. Shay was the connects daughter, and there was no way he was gone be okay with Renegade treating her like shit. All of this shit

would have been for nothing, if we lose out on the shit

now. My ass wasn't going, and I felt we needed a

meeting with his ass. Waiting on Renegade and Greedy

to come over, I paced the floor until the bell rung.

Running over, I answered and let them in. This

nigga Greedy was out here in twenty-degree weather in

them damn Jesus sandals. I thought Jazzy made him get

rid of them mother fuckers. They walked to the kitchen,

and I started singing.

"Swing low, sweet chariot. Coming forth to carry

me home." They looked at me like I was crazy, and I

laughed and kept on singing. "Swing looowww, sweet

chariottttt coming forth to carry me home." Renegade

stopped in his tracks, like he thought I was losing my mind.

"Nigga what the fuck wrong with you. Why you singing that shit? Jada husk then flew up your nose and got you high or some shit?" Laughing, we sat down at the table.

"Walk with me Lord, walk with me. Walk with me Lord, walk with me. While I'm on this, tedious journey I want Jesus to walk with me." Renegade stopped laughing. He thought I was losing my mind.

"Nigga straight up, fuck is wrong with you? You converted or some shit? You been to church, I'm lost than a mother fucker."

"Nigga, you ain't look down at Greedy feet? His ass a disciple again, and every step his ass took had me feeling churchy." Renegade looked down, and his nose turned up quick.

"Greedy, did you get them mother fuckers out the garbage? How the fuck you get them bitches back? Your ass walking home, I'm not going outside with you in them fucking shoes. Looking like a fucking freedom fighter. I'm sick of this shit." Renegade actually looked pissed, and I couldn't stop laughing.

"Fuck yall. They my house shoes. Jazzy agreed to let me wear them in the house. These bitches comfortable."

"She said in the house, but you got your dumb ass outside walking on water. Let's do this conference call to see what it is." Renegade grabbed his phone and dialed the connect.

"Renegade is there a problem at the border?" His ass always had this I'm better than thou ass tone.

"Everything is good boss. I'm calling because your daughter showed up here, and brought a bunch of mess to my doorstep saying me and you had problems if I didn't comply with her. I'm just trying to see where we stood." You could hear him take a deep breath, and I thought it was about to be some bullshit.

"We are good as long as my money is good. I also explained this to my daughter. There is no bad blood between us over you and her personal issues. Now if you will excuse me, I have more pressing things to attend to. Business is a go as usual." This bitch ass nigga hung up, but he told us what we needed to hear.

"That bitch not only fucking with my household, but she lied. That let's me know she could be lying about everything including the baby." His ass was trying to convince his self.

"You just don't want that damn Pitbull to be your baby. Nigga you ain't slick. Yall can leave though, now that I know my money is good, I need some pussy."

"Lai might not give me none until the results are back. I'm mad as hell they come back day before Valentine's Day."

"It's been two weeks, so at least you will know. Just buy her something really nice. Some roses or something." This nigga Greedy had no game.

"Nigga, roses? He done had a deerbra, his ass better buy her a planet. She gotta walk around with that uglass baby. You got too much money to be that damn cheap." Laughing, they headed out the door, and I went upstairs to find Jada. She was lying in the bed naked and half sleep. Pulling my clothes off, I climbed in and slid my dick straight to my favorite spot.

"Spread that shit for me girl." Not even thinking twice, she opened her legs up and let daddy's dick right in.

"Did you check on the baby."

"The baby been sleep, now I need you to swallow these other kids for me. Can you do that?" Nodding her head, I started deep stroking all in that gushy shit. My baby walls were gripping the shit out of me.

"Turn over and move to the end of the bed." Doing what I asked, I pushed down on her back and arched that mother fucker. Her ass in the air had me

hard as fuck, until I felt a sharp ass pain in my shin.

Blood was trickling down my leg and shit.

"Jada, I know your mother fucking feet didn't just

cut me? Get the fuck up. Move. You got ten minutes to

go get dressed and go get your feet done, or I'm buying

your ass goat cheese for Valentine's Day. Shit don't

make no damn sense." My hoe had blades on her damn

feet, and I was sick of this shit. "Find me some damn

ointment."

SHAY...

Waiting on these tests had a bitch nervous as hell.

If Renegade wasn't the father, I was gone be looking

stupid as fuck. I thought we would be able to talk while

we got swabbed, but he brought his damn guard dog of

a bitch with him.

She must be intimidated, and she better be. I'm

working on being alone with him right now, and I

promise once I do, his ass is mine. He knows what this

pussy is like, and as mad as she is, I know she ain't giving

him none. Calling his phone, I hoped he answered.

When he picked up, I did my happy dance.

"What the fuck you want Shay? I told you we ain't

got shit to talk about until the tests come back." Trying

to stay composed, I spoke calmly.

"I know, but I think you will regret it once the

results come back and you didn't even try to bond with

him. Can you just come over and meet him? I'm not

trying to fuck up your family, but your son is now a part of that family." He got quiet, and I can tell he was thinking about it.

"I don't want to get attached to something that may not be mine. I think it's best if we just wait until the results Shay."

"I get that, and I'm not trying to force you. Just at least come meet him. You can't get attached from one meeting. I came all the way this way for you to meet your son, and you won't even look at him." More silence.

"Where are you staying?" After giving him my hotel and room number, I jumped my ass in the shower. The truth is, the baby has three possible daddies. Renegade's time just match up more. Rolling with time, and my gut, I knew he had to be the daddy. He wouldn't

deny him once I got my mouth on his dick. Jumping out

the water, I put on a see through fitted dress, and

waited for him to come. After about twenty minutes,

there was a knock on my door. When I opened it, you

could see in his face that he wanted me.

"Shay, what the fuck are you on? I'm not on that, I

came here to see the baby." Smiling, I walked away

letting my ass jiggle.

"You've never been around me outside of the

shop. This is how I walk around my shit. I know why

you're here, and he is over there in the bed." Walking

over to the bed, he picked up the baby and just stared.

"What's his name?"

"Shemar. Make sure you hold his head." When he tried to do it right, I walked over to him and showed him the right way. My nipple made a mistake and brushed his lip. Of course, I did it on purpose, but I pretended I didn't. It hardened from his touch, and I could feel my pussy leaking already. Moving back slowly, I watched him try to bond with him. You could see it was hard for him, but he would get used to it.

Sitting across from him, I made sure my pussy was visible and there for the taking. All he had to do was come get this shit, and it was all his.

"See, it's not that hard. He just need to get used to your scent and touch." As if the baby was on my side, he started crying. Feeling his pamper, I knew he wanted his diaper changed. Taking him from Renegade, I laid him on the bed, and cleaned him up. Making sure I bent

over enough where he got a good view of this ass and

my pussy, I bounced harder than I needed to, so it could

shake. Putting the baby toward the middle of the bed, I

walked over to where Renegade was sitting.

"Are you okay?"

"It's a lot to take in. Let me use your bathroom

right quick." Giving him the okay, I smiled when I saw his

hard on through his jeans. I knew I was getting to him,

and I was about to go in for the kill. Making sure I left

enough time pass so he could have it out, I walked in the

bathroom.

"Shay what the fuck are you doing? I'll be out in a

minute." Dropping to my knees, I grabbed his dick and

started stroking it. You could see he was fighting with his

self. Closing his eyes, he put his head back. As soon as my mouth hit his dick, I deep throated it. Knowing there was no way he was nutting that fast, I pulled my mouth back. Aiming his dick, he continued to piss all over me. Trying to get up, he pushed my ass back to the floor and continued to relieve his self all over my fucking face and body.

"Are you crazy?" I was trying to go off, but had to stop so no more piss wouldn't go in my mouth. It seemed like this nigga pissed forever.

"Don't try to run now. This had to be what the fuck you wanted. If a nigga pissing and you put your mouth on his dick, you must have wanted that golden shower. Hoes like you love that shit huh? Well here you go bitch, take it all." Once he was done, his ass actually had the nerve to shake the shit, and put his dick up. Washing his hands, he stepped over me and walked out. Finally, able to get up, I ran behind him.

"You fucked with the wrong bitch. As soon as I tell my father, your ass is through. You got five minutes to meet me in the shower and make this shit right, or your ass is done." The nigga actually laughed.

"Bitch please, I already talked to your father. Your idle threats don't mean shit to me. Don't contact me again. I'll holla at you when the results come back. Pissy ass bitch." His dog ass walked out of my door singing R. Kelly. If I was a nigga I would have beat his ass. I'm praying this baby is his. Once it says it is, I'm going to make him and his bitch life hell.

My ass gone be the worse baby mama he ever came across. Nigga think he can walk all over me, and treat me like shit. Renegade had another thing coming. His Valentine's Day was about to be hell.

LAILA...

"Today you had a visitor, or should I say an old friend. But wait a minute, that's not where it ends no. Is there something that you wanna tell me, cus I'm believing what your friend say bout your hidden secrecy. Girlfriend, she wasn't disrespectful in fact she's a hundred percent sure, and how could I argue with her holding a baby with eyes like yours. SHE SAID IT'S YOUR CHILD.

My ass was sitting here screaming and trying to sing *Your Child by Mary J. Blige.* Waiting on the test was driving me crazy. Don't get me wrong, I know the shit was before my time. It still bothered me though. I'm not cut out to take care of someone else's child. Some women just ain't built like that, and I'm one. My ass is selfish, and I can admit that. The only baby I wanted him to have was my baby girl. We came in this marriage with no kids, and I wanted it to stay that way.

His ass been trying to get some, but of course that shit ain't happening. We both been walking around with attitudes. My ass been waiting for him to come home though, because my body had different plans. I've been hornier than a mother fucker for the past few hours.

Pussy just jumping.

His ass said he had to go handle some business, and I was praying the shit didn't take all night. If he waited too long, my ass would end up falling asleep. Grabbing my phone, I decided to call Jada and Jazzy. Hoping they ass was woke, the babies kept they ass going to bed early. It was funny because they both had boys. Now they just waiting on my ass to pop. Calling Jada first, you could tell she was on her way to sleep.

"Bitch now you know it's bed time. What you want?"

"Call Jazzy first. I need to talk shit. You hoes can stay woke for me, I have done way more for yall ass."

Smacking her lips, her line went silent. I knew she was

calling her on three- way.

"Jazzy wake your ass up, Lai cry baby ass is on the

phone. She wants to talk, and apparently, it can't wait

until tomorrow." This hoe got on my fucking nerves

sometimes.

"Yall, what if the baby is his? I can't be a step

mom. That shit ain't in me, and I know if I want to stay

married, I would have to."

"You ain't lying, and Quan told me how ugly the

baby is. Take a strong woman to do that shit. Couldn't

be me, I would kill his ass." I agreed with Jada because

that's how the fuck I felt.

"Greedy too cheap to get another mother fucker

pregnant. His ass barely wants to buy milk for our baby.

Yet, his ass can keep buying these ugly ass sandals." We all laughed, but they weren't helping me.

"Yall think Renegade will leave me if I told him his baby couldn't come in my house?" They ass stayed silent, and I knew the answer. That nigga was gone be ghost.

"Lai, why you tripping over shit when you don't even know what it is. You got two days to figure out if he the father or not. Cross that fucking bridge when you get there. Right now, I need her ass to get off the phone. You know she like to rub her feet against shit when she talks." This bitch had me on speaker phone and Quan was there.

"Wait, if Renegade had to handle some business, why are you home? Shouldn't you be out there too?"

"Lai, he the boss. It's shit he have to do sometimes that don't include us. He got workers and shit out there. He probably collecting money. Quit worrying so much and go your ass the fuck to bed." Smacking my lips, I hung up the phone.

Fuck them, they ass always act like I'm overreacting. Let it be their asses, all hell would break loose. Knowing I couldn't do shit but wait it out these two days, I hated that the shit was coming before Valentine's Day. Might fuck my entire shit up.

Hearing the garage, I knew he was home, and I could get this pussy played in. As soon as he walked in, I grabbed his dick letting him know what time it was.

"Hold on baby, I been out there in the streets. Let me shower first then you can get this dick. Your ass better be wet already when I get out." Climbing in bed, I

started playing in my pussy waiting for him to join me.

My phone went off, and I grabbed it thinking it was Jada.

Looking at my phone, I didn't know who it was.

713-879-6587 If you're wondering where your man was, he was just here with our son. Before he left he played in this pussy, and now he is coming home to you. I would suggest you don't kiss him. His mouth been all over my body.

The bitch had the nerve to even send a picture. This nigga had the nerve to be in the shower, trying to wash her off. I was about to beat the fuck out of his ass. Not responding to her, I refused to give her the satisfaction that she bothered me. As soon as he walked out, I went in on his ass.

"I hope you ready for this dick, I'm about to change your life." Grabbing the lamp, I threw it at his ass.

"You thought you was gone go be with that bitch and then come home to me? Nigga you got me fucked up. We are done, get your shit and get the fuck out of my house." Looking like he wasn't about to budge, I tried to pick up the night stand.

"Lai put that shit down before you fuck around and hurt the baby. Let me explain." Running towards him, I punched him wherever my fist landed.

"Explain what? How you lied to me about where the fuck you were going. How you were over there playing with that ugly ass baby. You fucked that bitch, and you think I'm dumb. Get the fuck out of my house

Rashaun." Storming off, you could tell he was pissed.

Grabbing his pants, he walked back over to me with his

phone. Pressing play, I heard the entire conversation

between him and Shay.

"She called me telling me how I didn't even

attempt to meet him. I'm not gone lie, I've been feeling

bad because what if he is my son? I treated his ass like

dog shit, and that shit wasn't cool no matter what the

situation was. I knew you wasn't gone understand the

shit, so I lied, and I'm sorry.

I should have told you what I was doing. When I

went to the bathroom she ran in there and threw her

mouth on my dick. I don't give a fuck about that bitch.

She been trying to fuck me since I met her, but I ain't

want her ass. The only reason I fucked her was to get

back at Megan for fucking her. I don't want that bitch. I

pissed all in her mouth, and on her ass. As you can

hear." Snatching his phone back, he walked off and

started packing a bag.

"Nigga you don't get to leave. You fucked up. You

put yourself in a fucked up situation, and that's on you.

You lied to your wife to go see a bitch about a dog, and

that is on you. How the fuck the bitch mouth get on your

dick that fast, you could have stopped it. Your ass

wanted to piss on her, and you allowed her to do it.

THAT IS ON YOU. So don't stand your big ass in here and

try to play victim. You could have avoided all this shit

had you talked to your wife.

Even though I would have been pissed, I would

have understood. I would have came with you, and

mugged the entire time, but none of this would have

happened. You can sleep in the guest room. Before you

lay down though, you better have me some butter

pecan ice cream with pickle juice on top. Thank you."

Walking off, I climbed in the bed.

"So now you not about to give me no pussy? I

ain't even do shit, why the fuck am I in trouble. This

some bullshit. I should bring your ass rocky road. "

"Your ass shouldn't have lied, and you better bring

me what the fuck I asked for." Laughing, he walked out

of the room. I knew he was going to bring me what I

wanted, because he went out of his way every night to

make sure I was straight. I couldn't wait for these tests

to come back. My life needed to get back on track, and

the shit needed to happen fast.

RENEGADE...

I couldn't believe this bitch Shay was really trying to fuck my shit up. I had the good mind to go back to her room, and spread her thoughts all over the fucking bed. Even though her dad said he was staying out of it, I knew he wouldn't take kindly to me killing his daughter. Since he knew what was going on, he would know it was my ass that did it. She knew damn well what she was on when she invited me over, but I'm smarter than a fifth grader. Something told me to record that shit, and that it might come in handy.

I just didn't know she would try to send shit to my wife and shit. That hoe was pushing my buttons, and was about to bring the savage out of my ass. Snatching my keys, I jumped in the whip and headed to the store to get this nasty ass shit she wanted. I couldn't wait until she had this damn baby. Laughing at the shit she had me getting, wifey gets what wifey wants.

****

Looking at the time, I been waiting for these damn results to hit my email. A nigga ain't never been so nervous in my life. Every guy wanted a son, but I ain't want one outside my damn marriage. This would ruin me and Lai, and I wasn't about to have that shit. No matter what the test said, I wasn't telling her ass until after Valentine's Day. We were going to enjoy our day, and I wasn't with the shit. My ringing phone brought me

out of my thoughts.

"Hey nigga is the puppy yours or nah? You got a

nigga over here waiting to see if he gone be bow wow's

uncle. Quit holding the tea as the bitches say." Quan

stayed on bullshit, but I was too nervous for his jokes.

They rolled right off my ass.

"The tea nigga? That shit sound extra suspect. I'm

waiting on the results now. My ass so nervous I got the

fucking bubble guts. Lai keep walking up looking at me

trying to see if I got them and shit."

"Nigga we all waiting. We been on face time half

the damn morning, so we could hear the shit together.

Your ass playing and shit."

"Nigga I'm not playing, but I'm not telling Lai until after tomorrow. I need some damn pussy, and nobody can turn down sex on Valentine's Day."

"You right about that. Did you get her gift?"

"Yea, it's being customized. I can get it in the morning. Nigga, what if this baby is mine bruh. I can't deal with that shit. Lai is going to beat my ass."

"Let me find out your ass a victim. You better fight back, or blink when we around so we know you need help. You don't have to take that shit you know. It's help out there for niggas like you. You do know Jesus is on the main line. Call Greedy and ask his ass for help." We fell out laughing, when my email buzzed off. Looking, it was the results, and my ass was scared as hell to open the shit.

"Nigga they here."

"Well open it shit. What it say?"

****

It was Valentine's Day, and I planned on making my wife's day a special one. She been stressing so hard lately, I needed her to know how I felt about her. After making her breakfast, I took it upstairs and sat the plate on the bed.

"Baby, Happy Valentine's Day." Kissing her on her pretty ass lips, she finally woke up. Her ass was glowing, and I fell in love with her every day all over again.

"Did you get the results baby?" I know it's been bothering her, since that's the first thing out of her mouth.

"Today is about you. Eat your breakfast so I can give you your gift. I put you some pickles on there too just in case you wanted them on your pancakes."

"Okay. I'll be done in a little while. Check the email." Nodding, I got up and went downstairs. I hated keeping secrets from her, but I wanted today to be about us. I wanted her to enjoy herself because she wanted to. As soon as she was done, she came down.

Grabbing her hand, I put other one over her eyes. Leading her outside, I stood her right in front of her gift. When she opened her eyes, she was face to face with a white on black 2018 Bugatti Chiron. I think she forgot she was pregnant, her ass took off running. Her screams

let me know she loved the shit, and I was ready to take

this mother fucker for a ride.

"Come on get in. I don't want you driving until

after you have baby girl, but you can never have her in

here."

"Alright daddy, whatever you say. Your ass must

gone babysit a lot." Laughing, we climbed in and took

off. The power of the engine, had my dick brick hard.

From the look on Lai's face, I know it was having the

same effect on her ass as well. Pulling over, I gave her

the look and she knew what it was. Grabbing my dick

out of my pants, Lai took her leggings off and climbed on

top of me. It felt like forever since I been inside of her

pussy, them two weeks almost killed a nigga.

"You better ride this shit, and your ass better not miss a fucking beat." Getting her good rhythm going, my baby started going ham on this mother fucker. Not about to let her get the best of me, I grabbed her waist and tore into that pussy.

"Baby slow down. Hold on." Not about to let her stop before I get my nut, I kept banging that shit. "Baby, wait." She started pushing away from me, and I could now see the pain on her face.

"Lai what's wrong?"

"Nigga I'm in labor. Let me up, and drive this mother fucker." Rushing her to the hospital, I broke that bitch in. By the time we walked in the door, she was screaming like a mother fucker. I couldn't believe she was having our baby on Valentine's Day. This shit would always be special to the both of us. The doctor's kept

telling her she needed to calm down because her

pressure was up. Climbing in bed with her, I knew

exactly how.

"Baby, you are going to be a great mom. I love you

so much, and you are going to do okay. Calm down so

that you don't stress the baby. I promise it's going to be

okay, and I'm not going anywhere. I got you a present."

Handing her a paper, she looked at the paper and tears

fell from her eyes.

"I knew that ugly ass puppy couldn't be yours.

Thank you baby, I love you so much." This day couldn't

have been any more perfect.

I GOTTA BE HIS

VALENTINE

REASON NUMBER 9

"I gotta be the one you touch. Baby, I gotta be the one you love. I gotta be the one you feel. I gotta be the one to fill your life with sunshine. I gotta be the one you know, cause I will always love you so. I gotta be the one you need, I'm just telling you that I gotta be." I Gotta Be-Jagged Edge

JEREMY...

You would think that my love life would be the shit, since I'm a professional ball player. That was not the case. All I had were a bunch of fly by nights, and the shit was getting old. I wanted someone in my life, and the shit just wasn't happening. The only chicks I

attracted were chicks who wanted bottle service for the

night, topped off with dick and doughnuts in the

morning. The type of money I was making, this big ass

house, and my career. You would think I could find a

decent ass chick. Especially in Cleveland. Who knew it

was so many gold diggers in this lil ass city.

Hanging out with Tre and Kira didn't make the shit

any better. Them mother fuckers were the happiest

couple alive, and his ass had to be my best friend. The

only joy I got out of being around them, was my God

son. TJ was funny as hell, and I couldn't wait to have a

kid of my own. He makes fatherhood look easy as hell.

Normally, I would be okay with being by myself,

but it was almost Valentine's Day. Everywhere I turned,

the shit reminded me that my ass was alone. Even Dee

hoe ass had somebody. How the fuck Latoya Nicole let

that happen was beyond me. That bitch fucked

everybody under the sun, and hurt a lot of people. Yet,

her ass was living her happily ever after.

Grabbing my gym bag, I headed to work off some

steam. Tre was supposed to be meeting me there. This

nigga had an entire gym in his house, but it was

something about being at an actual gym that got your

shit flowing. Jumping in my Porsche, I drove fast through

the city.

When I walked in, I was guessing everybody had

the same idea today. They ass must be trying to get fit,

so they could look good for this janky ass holiday. Damn

near all the machines were taken, and a nigga couldn't

even do his cardio. Seeing a treadmill open up, I headed over. Until this chick walked up and took it.

"Excuse me, I was about to get on that." Looking at me, she smiled and kept right on walking.

"Maybe if you came here more often, you wouldn't have been as slow. Tone it up chubby." Looking down at myself, I knew her ass was lying. My shit was tight, and she had me fucked up.

"You can keep it, your ass jiggling out of control and them dents need to be worked out. Good luck." Instead of her getting offended, she laughed.

"This mother fucker doing the Harlem Shake ain't it? I may be a little out of shape, but I see you looking." Not being able to argue with her there, I reached over and increased her speed.

"You gone need to go a little faster to work on them dents. Let me know when you're done, I'm not trying to be arguing with fat people all day." Smiling at her, I walked off and started on the weight bench. Tre walked in, and once he walked over, the people started to realize who we were. Guess they had to see the both of us together in order for them to figure it out.

"Nigga we should have worked out at my house. How we gone get a sweat going if we gotta keep stopping to give autograph? This is turning into a publicity event." Agreeing, I tried to act like I didn't see all the cameras flashing.

"Hey chubby, the treadmill is open." Seeing the girl from earlier standing there all sweaty and shit, had me lusting like a mother fucker. Tre looked at me trying to figure out what was going on with the exchange.

"You know her?" Smiling, I shook my head no.

"But I'm about to." Following her over to the treadmill, I couldn't keep my eyes off her ass. It's not that it was big, the shit was just perfect. She had a toned workout body. Not thick, but not skinny. Just toned. Her breast looked like a B cup, but they heaved up and down perfectly. When I climbed on, she got on the one next to me. Made me feel like she didn't want to be away from a nigga.

"What's your name? Since we're stuck being work out partners."

"Misha, but we're not about to do that. We can cut the shit now. You're not my type, and I'm not looking. No need to waste your tired ass game, use your breath to keep up. You're slacking." A nigga was damn near appalled that she was shooting me down. Shit like that just didn't happen when you were a ball player. Bitches threw that pussy like an alley hoop.

"Who said I was trying to talk to you. I just asked your name. Who the hell done pissed in your cheerios?"

"I know who you are, and I'm not into that lifestyle. Actually, I'm not into men at this moment." She knew who I was. I smiled as I continued to run. "Why the hell you over there grinning?"

"Because you know who I am." Shrugging my shoulders, I continued to run. Seeing her grab her belongings, I actually started to panic. "You leaving?"

"Unlike you, I get out early and do what I need to. I've been here for a few hours. You got it though, just remember to put one foot in front of the other. You'll be fine." Her ass walked off without giving me a second thought. Didn't even look back. Tre walked over laughing.

"You done fell off. Nigga don't even know how to get a number no more. Did you at least get her name?"

"Yea, I got it, and that's all her ass was trying to give up. I'll see her again." I would most definitely see her again.

TRE…

"Baby, where your fine ass at?" The only thing that stayed on my mind, was my wife and kid. They were my fucking life, and a nigga knew he was blessed. My career wouldn't be where it was if it wasn't for her.

"Tre, she went out with some of the girls. I'm not sure which players, all yall look the same." I had no idea who the hell she was with. Kira didn't really get along with the player's wives because of Dee. They all loved her hoe ass, and as long as she was around, Kira stayed away.

I'm confused as to what the fuck my wife would be doing with them. This shit sounded like a set up to me, and I wasn't about to let nobody come in between my shit again. I had to get to the bottom of this, and I was going to do that shit fast. It seems like my wife

forgot what that bitch took us through.

"Ma, where is TJ? I know she ain't take him with

her."

"He upstairs in his room. Calm down son. I can see

that you are upset, but they are family. I told her she

could at least go and hear her out." Now I was ready to

curse her ass out. I know she was Kira's mother, but I

was not about to allow her to do this shit.

"I'm trying to say this in the least disrespectful

way possible. Stay out of our marriage. I know you

allowed a lot of stuff to happen in your life, but I won't

allow Kira to be that person. Dee tried to tear through

our fucking family, and you want her to be okay with

that. Ain't that much forgiveness in the world. Now if

you will excuse me, I'm about to call my wife and tell her to bring her ass the fuck home." Walking off, it took everything in me not to end that shit with a bitch. How dare she try and guilt Kira into talking to that girl? I'm shocked that Kira listened. Grabbing my phone, I called her.

"Hey baby. What your fine ass doing?" Just from how she sounded, I could tell she was drunk. This was a disaster waiting to happen. Kira ass doesn't drink, and I knew she didn't know how to handle her liquor.

"Get your ass home right now. If I have to come get you, we are going to have a problem."

"Dang hubby, loosen up." She was about to piss me off.

"Kira, don't make me come get you. Tell your lil friends you have to go. Your ass better not drive either. Take a fucking Uber." Not even giving her the chance to respond, I hung the phone up. Her ass had me three fifty hot, and if she knew what was best, her ass better be on her way the fuck home. We needed to talk about this shit before I left tomorrow for our away game. I didn't want to leave with unresolved issues, but at the end of the day, this was one thing I wasn't bending on.

Thirty minutes later, she came staggering in the door. If I was a woman beater, I would have slapped her ass. She was being extra as fuck too.

"Kira, why the fuck are you hanging out with Dee? You know better, and you know what the fuck she stands for." When she put her finger up to my lip to shush me, I started to bite that shit off. Issa nubby.

"Calm down. You stress too much. It's okay, we just had drinks. Nothing happened. My mother thought we should work on our problems, and I'm glad we did. We had a good time tonight." Even though her words were slurred, they cut deep. How could she even consider being cool with her?

"If you choose to hang with her, then you will lose me. You can decide what's more important. I'll sleep in the guest room tonight." Not giving her a chance to rebuttal, I walked out. I know she was drunk, but I'm sure she heard that ultimatum loud and clear.

****

Waking up the next morning, I hoped Kira picked

wisely. She knew that girl shouldn't be nowhere near

any of us, and there was no way I would allow her to be

cool with her ass. After handling my hygiene, I went

downstairs to cook breakfast. Whenever I had an away

game, I would always cater to my wife before I left. After

I got everything started, I pulled my phone out to check

the scores from the games last night. I did this every day,

it was my way of keeping up with the competition.

I damn near choked on my own spit when I saw

the headlines from last night. Checking every website

possible, I knew the world saw it when I saw it on TMZ.

It was a picture of Kira kissing another man at the bar.

The shit was everywhere, and I was about to drag her

ass everywhere. As I was walking up the stairs, her mom came running in.

"Tre calm down. We don't know what happened. The shit could be photo shopped." My ass almost drew my foot back and drop kicked her down the stairs.

"Ma, if you don't mind I would like to talk to my wife alone. This is your fault, and I knew being around her was trouble. Just stay the fuck out of our marriage." Running up the stairs, I bust in our room causing her to jump up. Holding her head, she looked like she was out of it.

"What time is it? How did I end up here?" You could tell she was really lost, and I didn't understand how her ass didn't remember.

"Kira, what happened last night?"

"I don't know. I went to meet Dee because my mama kept talking about family, and I needed to hear her out at least. Do it for her. When I got there, she had already ordered drinks. Because of the tension, I drunk one down. Now I'm here." Pulling up the headlines on my phone, I showed it to her.

"You don't remember him, but your tongue was down his throat? Your ass knew better, and there was no way you should have met up with her ass. This is on you, and I don't know if we can fix this shit."

"Baby I'm sorry, I don't even know what happened. Fuck, I shouldn't have drunk anything. I didn't mean for any of this to happen."

"No, you're wrong, you shouldn't have been there in the first fucking place. I have to go to my away game, we will talk about this when I get back. If I come back."

Grabbing my luggage, I walked out of the door. My life

just went from perfect to shit.

DEE...

In order to have the life I wanted to live, I was still

married to Mouse. My mom had passed away six

months ago, and he was all I had. No money, no job, so I

wasn't giving up my stability because he was ugly as shit,

and it wasn't gone change. Instead, I cheated my ass off.

Once a hoe, always a hoe and that shit wasn't gone

change. His ass be out on the road too much to even

notice.

Knowing how my auntie felt about my mama, and family. I used that against her, so she could persuade Kira to come out with me. We needed to bury the hatch, but not for the reasons that she thought. With me and Kira beefing, I had no access to Tre. His ass avoided me like the plague, and I needed that shit to end.

Hell yea, I w as still on that bullshit. He was the big score I needed to be set for life. If I could get him to fuck me raw again, I could get pregnant, and I would be set for life. My ass wouldn't have to deal with Mouse ugly ass no more and I could fuck who I wanted without sneaking. That was the ultimate come up, and I was determined to get it.

Once I knew Kira was coming, I ordered our drinks ahead of time. She wasn't a drinker and one cup would put her on her ass. Slipping a x pill in her shit, I knew her

ass was gone be down for whatever. I was about to end

her ass, and all she would want to do was run far away

from here. There was no way Tre would stay with her,

after I was done with her ass tonight.

Giving some money to the nigga, and chick that

was going to end her life, I waited on her ass to walk in.

Once the drug kicked in, they were going to take her to a

room for a threesome, and I was gone make sure I had

all the pictures. When she walked in the door, her ass

was acting like she didn't want to be there and downed

the drink. That was even better. By the time I got out my

fake ass apology, the drugs had taken affect.

She was up on the dance floor damn near grinding

on anybody who would let her. Giving the nod to the

flunky I paid, he approached her. Not even speaking one word, he slid his tongue in her mouth and her ass was kissing him back like he was her nigga. Pulling my phone out, I got some good ass pics. He was gripping her ass, and everything. Knowing it was time to get out of there, he led her to the car, and we all made our way to the hotel.

As soon as we walked in the door, he pushed her on the bed and had her pussy in his mouth. The girl flunky started massaging her breast, and I was the picture girl. Even though her ass was drunk as hell, her ringing phone halted all that shit. She knew it was Tre, and she jumped up to answer it.

After she hung up, her ass didn't say a word. She ran out of there like he was her damn daddy. I've had the dick, so I would have too. Why fuck someone else, when you had all that at home. It didn't matter to me, because the pics that I had was enough. The shit was about to hit the fan, and I was about to finally get my man.

****

After leaking the pics of the kiss, I knew Tre would be pissed. His ass don't know it was about to get a lot worse. Mouse was leaving out for his away game, so I knew where Tre was about to be. They just didn't know I was about to be there as well.

Getting my shit together, and packing my sexy shit, I headed to the airport and got ready to go get my man. The flight was short, and sweet. My ass was probably just overtly excited, and I had a burst of

energy.

When I got to the hotel, I gave the girl at the desk

a thousand dollars to give me Tre's key card. Once inside

his room, I changed into my sexy shit, and hid all my

stuff in the closet. He was in for a surprise, and I was

about to get that dick.

When he walked in the room, I had all the pics

spread out across the bed. Sitting on top of them, I

played in my pussy waiting for him to look up. As soon

as he saw me, he blew out a breath. Not as mad as he

usually is, I knew it was because of the leaked pics.

"Dee, I'm really not in the mood for your shit. You

have done enough. Please leave out of my room before I

call the cops." Taking off his jacket, he went to the bar

and poured a drink.

"You might want to look at these pics before you

put me out. Might do you good to have some tit for tat

sex."

"What the fuck are you talking about?" Picking up

some of the pics, I handed them to him. Seeing the tears

well up in his eyes as he looked them over, I knew I had

him where I wanted him. He was so stuck looking at the

pics, he didn't even realize I was massaging his dick. The

mother fucker got hard though, and that's all I needed.

Taking advantage of his hurt, I unzipped his pants and

pulled it out. Stroking it, I wanted him to be brick hard

before I deep throated him. Nothing was better than a

big ass, hard ass dick hitting your tonsils.

"Dee, you can let my dick go. I'm not drunk, and I'm not that desperate. You can let yourself out." Trying to change his mind, I started stroking for dear life. You could tell he really didn't have any fight, but pussy was the last thing on his mind. Grabbing my hand, he didn't even get mean about it. All he did was try to remove it.

Not caring that I was staring at a broken man, I knew he wasn't strong enough to stop me, I kept stroking.

"Dee, I'm really trying not to kill you and it would be good for you to leave. All of this is because of you, and the only thought that's going through my mind is breaking your neck. Sex is not there, and bitch if you know what's best for you, I'm asking you to get the fuck out of my room." Hearing the tone of his voice, I knew he was dead serious. Before I could hall ass out of there, Kira walked in. Taking my hand off his dick, I prayed she listened to what was going on. I didn't want Tre to kill me.

"This is why you picked a fight with me? Nigga we back here again, you got me fucked up." This time, Tre didn't try to explain. He handed her the pictures. The look on her face was priceless.

"What the fuck is this? When was this, Tre, I have no idea what the fuck is going on." His eyes were cold as hell, and I almost felt bad for her. Almost.

"Kira, get out of my room. When I make it home, I want you out of my house. We will discuss visitation for TJ. Please don't make me ask you again." I'm guessing she knew his ass wasn't playing either, because she turned around and left. Knowing he was pissed at her,

and leaving, I just knew I was about to get the dick.

"Dee, you got five seconds. Don't test me."

Walking away from me, he went in the bathroom and

closed the door. I got the fuck out of there and made my

exit.

JEREMY...

When it was time to head to the airport, I went to

Tre's room to see if he was ready to go. My nigga

opened the door looking like shit. Not drunk, just

broken.

"Fuck is wrong with you?" Never responding, he handed me the pics. Something had to be wrong, there was no way Kira would cheat on him.

"Where did you get these from? I'm not sure I believe this shit."

"Dee gave them to me last night. She was here trying to fuck. As usual. I can say one thing, that hoe is persistent. After all these years, you would think her hoe ass would find another target."

"Tell me you didn't fuck her." Nigga shot me a death look.

"Nigga please, I hate that hoe with my entire being. She has successfully ruined us. Man, I want to have that bitch killed so bad."

"You sure you want to take the word of her hoe

ass? Shit ain't adding up, how did she get the pics?"

Shrugging his shoulders, he grabbed his bags ready to

walk out. Not wanting to get in the middle of that shit, I

left it alone. Ray Charles could see it was something way

off with this shit, but he had to see it on his own. Right

now, he was hurt, but he would eventually see that shit.

Dee was up to something as usual, and it was a

damn shame this bitch was still at it. She needed to grow

the fuck up, or somebody was gone kill her nasty ass.

Both of us rode in silence to the airport.

Boarding the plane, I almost passed out when I

saw Misha was one of the stewardess. This is what she

did for a living. Her ass was looking fine as hell in her

blue suit. She hadn't even noticed me, and I was staring her ass down.

"I knew I would see you again. Is this your last flight?" She turned around and smiled.

"Your ass is a stalker. Yes, this is my last one. Good game last night by the way."

"Thank you. Why don't we quit acting like we not attracted to each other, and go get something to eat when our plane land. We both know all you gone do is give my ass some peanuts." Laughing, her expression softened.

"Okay, if that will stop you from following me around." Heading to my seat, a nigga was happy as hell. If all went well on this dinner, I won't be alone on Valentine's Day. I just hoped my nigga Tre wasn't trading places with me. The shit looked bad, but I know Dee. His

ass better do his homework first, or her hoe ass was

going to win.

Knowing I had a date, the flight seemed to take

forever, but we finally landed. I wasn't getting off this

plane without making sure Misha ass was going with me

after.

"I'm about to go home and get my car. Put your

number in my phone, and I will come pick you up in an

hour. Is that good for you?"

"Yes, that's fine." Grabbing my phone, she put her

number in. Walking away, my ass couldn't stop my lips

from curling up. I was smiling hard as fuck, until the

reporters bombarded us.

"Tre, is there trouble in paradise between you and your wife? The recent pictures that are circulating the web, indicates that she may be cheating." You could see Tre was ready to catch a case, pushing him along, I saved him from doing something stupid.

"Look, I know you're hurting. All I'm saying is, find out the facts first before you do something you will regret. We are talking about Dee. Just remember that."

"Fuck all that, I need you to take a quick ride with me. If I'm not gone be happy, that bitch ain't either. You can believe that shit." Knowing I only had an hour, I was gone be pushing it. This shit here, was too good to resist. It was time that hoe got what the fuck she deserved.

Jumping in the car with Tre, we headed to Mouse's crib, and I couldn't wait to see the look on her face when we fucked her world up.

Knocking on the door, Mouse ugly ass had made it home and opened the door. I don't know why Tre didn't tell him at the airport. I guess he wanted Dee ass to be here as well.

"Damn niggas. I just saw yall, can a nigga get some pussy?"

"Speaking of pussy, where your girl at?" Tre went in for the kill, and I was happy. We needed to hurry up so I could get to my date.

"She upstairs, why you looking for Dee? Hey Dee, come here for a minute"

"Wait until she comes down." The look on Dee's face was priceless when she hit the bottom of the stairs.

"Hey baby, what's up." She kept looking at Tre as if she was trying to convince him not to say anything.

"Okay, let's not beat around the bush. Your bitch broke up my marriage, and I thought you should know what the fuck she been up to. No matter how many times I try to tell her I'm not interested, she keeps trying to fuck.

She showed up at my hotel room laying in my bed, playing in her pussy. She took pics of my girl, and even though we are done, I thought you should know my dick was in her hands, and she was begging to put it down her throat. Just so you know, I put her ass out." You could tell Mouse was pissed, and Dee was looking for a

way out.

"Aight thank yall. I'll holla at yall niggas at

practice." We got up out of there, and I made that nigga

rush me to my car. I needed to get to my date.

TRE...

After busting up Dee's shit, I headed home. I

thought I would feel better after that, but the hurt was

still the same. I can't believe that this had become my

life. Kira was different from all the others, and I can't

believe she did that shit to me. After all we did to find

our way back to each other, how the fuck could she

allow that bitch to come back between us.

Walking in the door, I knew my day was about to get worse. Kira's mama was sitting on the couch looking like she was ready to fight.

"Is that why you didn't want Kira and Dee to get close again? Because you were still fucking her. You got a lot of nerve. Out of all the shit you took my daughter through, you don't even give her the benefit of the doubt.

God don't like ugly, and your ugly ass gone get yours. Damn dummy. You know damn well that girl ain't cheated on you. Now I don't know what happened, or how those pictures came about, but you know she didn't cheat on you. You can't be that damn stupid."

"Where is Kira?"

"She left, like you told her."

"Then you can get the fuck out and follow her. All of this came about because of you. If you hadn't forced her to go talk to that girl, then none of this would have happened. I'm not gone sit here and pretend that I'm happy to see you. I need to be alone, so I can think."

"I don't care how mad you are, you will not speak to me that way. I know now that it was a mistake, but that didn't give you the right to sleep with Dee. Now I'm not sure what happened, but the way I see it, yall are even. Now fix this shit before I beat your ass." She actually had the nerve to shoot out demands.

"The way I see it, you are over the line as usual. Tell Kira bring my son back, and then she can go. In the meantime, let yourself out please." Walking upstairs, I went to my room and cried. They say karma is a bitch, but I thought I had paid my dues. This was some pain, I

wouldn't wish on no nigga. Every time I think about it, I

want to hire somebody to kill the shit out of that bitch

Dee. She was like a fucking roach you couldn't get rid of.

My Valentine's Day was about to be fucked up,

when I was supposed to be laid up with my wife. How

the fuck was I supposed to function? This girl was my

world, and I don't even know if I could be without her.

For now, I was mad as hell, and nobody could change my

mind.

Hearing somebody come up the stairs, I knew it

was Kira. The fact that she didn't walk straight in our

room, let me know she put TJ down first. My heart was

pounding fast as hell waiting on her to come in. When I

saw the door opening, I closed my eyes and played

sleep. Feeling her body rub against me as she climbed over, had me nervous as hell. her small frame pushed up against me, and I had to fight the urge to hold her.

Kira's small hand started gliding up and down my chest, and I knew no matter how mad I was, if she kept this up, I was gone be inside of her. As soon as I felt her hand hit my dick, I knew it was over. No matter what, I would always be attracted to her. She pulled my dick out of my pants, and stroked it slow.

She stopped, and I could tell she was trying to get out of her clothes. Her mouth slid down on my dick, and I missed her so much. I couldn't believe she did this shit to us, and I ended up being pissed. Snatching her up, I forced her down on the bed. Climbing on top of her, I rammed my dick in not even caring if she was wet. I wanted this nut, but I needed her to hurt like I was.

Grabbing her around the neck, I squeezed the shit as

tight as I could as I fucked her like a bitch on the street.

Zoning out, I kept slamming until I felt my nut rising.

Shuddering, I released all of my seeds inside of her, and I

finally opened my eyes. My baby was sitting there crying

her eyes out, and the shit broke my heart. Laying down

beside her, I pulled her to me.

"I'm sorry Kira. I don't know what came over me.

No matter how I felt, I shouldn't have treated you like

that. I don't know how to deal with this, and a nigga

really don't know what to do. I had you on a pedestal for

so long, it's hard seeing you down here with the rest of

us fuck ups. I didn't sleep with Dee. When you walked in,

I had just threatened to kill her if she didn't get her

hands off me. Even though you broke me, I wouldn't do that to you." Leaning over, she looked at me.

"I know you didn't, because I know you and trust you. What hurts is that you don't trust me. I'm telling you I don't remember any of that, and I have no idea what happened. All I can say is I'm sorry, but I swear I wouldn't have done that." Listening to her, I could hear the sincerity in her voice. She really didn't remember.

"Baby, tell me what happened again."

"My mama told me Dee called saying we were the only family she had, and she really wanted to make up with me. My mama guilted me into going. When I got there, she already had a drink waiting for me on the table. Because it was an awkward silence, I downed the drink. That is the last thing I remember. I've been drunk, but never like that." Thinking how Dee just happened to

have the pictures let me know she was there. Shaking

my head, I realized she set Kira up.

"Baby girl, Dee drugged you. Nothing else makes

sense. That's how she had the pictures, she was

expecting the shit to happen. I swear I hate that bitch.

She is determined to break us the fuck up." We looked

at each other and laughed. The shit really wasn't funny,

but what else could we do in that situation.

"I'm so fucking stupid. I should have known

something was up. The hoe had the drinks sitting there

just waiting. I should whoop my mama ass." Now that, I

was in agreeance with.

"At the end of the day, we go through our shit,

but we always find our way back to each other. That hoe

can't break us, and from now on, we gotta promise to

always talk the shit out first. As long as that hoe is

around, we gone need to remember that shit."

"I'm beating that bitch to sleep when I catch her.

I'm sorry for going baby, that shit will never happen

again."

"I love you baby, and I always will."

"And I'll always love you back."

DEE...

My life just couldn't get any worse. The minute

Tre and Jeremy left the house, Mouse lit into my ass.

that nigga was mad as hell, and I couldn't think of a good

lie to tell to get my ass out of it.

"I should have known your bitch ass wasn't shit but another gold digger. I gave your ass everything, anything you asked for. Yet, that shit wasn't enough. You are the worse kind of bitch."

"Baby, how are you gone let him come in here and destroy what we have. You know damn well I don't want Tre. Come on baby, let's go upstairs and have sex."

"Not this time. My nigga wouldn't lie to me, and I could see the hurt in that nigga's eyes. Even if your ass was choosing to be a hoe, and cheat on me. You could have done that shit with a nigga I didn't know. Your ass crossed a line, and I'm done. Get the fuck out of my house." At least I could get my shit. My jewelry would alone would get me by until I found my next victim.

Going towards the stairs, I was about to head up, but he stopped me.

"Naw, your ass leaving here with what the fuck you came with. Nothing. Now get the fuck out of my shit." Stomping out of the door, I was going to leave for now, but I was coming back. His ugly ass was gone give in, all I had to do was suck his dick. He just need to calm down.

Scrolling through my phone, I wasn't paying attention as I crossed the street. Too busy looking for a nigga I could call, it was too late to move out of the way. The horn blowing told me exactly where I had fucked up at. The impact sent my ass soaring into the air, and I prayed God didn't allow me to die. This couldn't be my karma, was the last thought as my body hit the ground.

****

When I woke up, I was in the hospital. I was in there for three weeks before they transferred my ass to a home. When I woke up, the doctors explained to me that I was paralyzed from the waist down. A bitch should have been careful what she prayed for. My ass was too busy begging not to die, I should have asked to be able to walk after the shit was over.

Mouse came to see me, and I thought we were about to get back on track. His ass served me divorce papers, and kicked my bitch ass to the curb. He at least paid for me to stay in a home, and that is where I would permanently reside. My life was fucked up, and I couldn't blame nobody but myself. Why the fuck couldn't I just leave Tre alone? He made it clear as day that he didn't want my ass, and I could have been happy with my life. Mouse gave me everything, and now my ass had nothing.

Ironically, I was a hoe all my life, and now I would be a hoe the remainder of my stay here. The orderlies came in my room every night asking for head. The hoe in me couldn't resist it. It's like, I needed to feel like myself some kind of way. Half of my body didn't work, but I was in here trying to stay alive by sucking dick. This was the worst Valentine's Day in history. After the movie went off, I wheeled myself to my room, and got ready to go to bed. Or so I thought.

The fat ass orderly made his way to my room, and locked the door. Knowing what he wanted, I felt the tears well up in my eyes. His ass smelled like onions, and pine sol. It's like he knows he stank like a mother fucker, but since he wanted his dick sucked, he dipped the shit in pine sol.

Knowing this was my life, and I had nobody to thank but myself, I opened my mouth and let the funky dick fuck my tonsils back.

KIRA...

Today was Valentine's Day, and it was one of the happiest days of my life. Me and Tre couldn't be happier, and the bitch Dee was finally out of our hair. Now I know I shouldn't be happy at the fact that she was hurt, but I was happy she was out of our life. The bitch caused so much pain, we barely made it thru. Looking in the mirror, I checked myself out one last time before we headed out.

"Kira, you cannot get any prettier. Get your ass down here before we be late. Damn girl."

"I'm right here baby. I had to make sure I was matching your fly. Don't want you out here checking out no other bitches."

"You know I only have eyes for you. Let's go, Jeremy and his girl waiting on us." We were heading out to see Fifty Shades Freed, and I couldn't wait. I was over the top and couldn't wait to watch my fine ass white man Christian Grey.

"I see you lusting over that nigga in your mind. I'll take your ass to see Jumanji. Don't play with me. Now let's get out of here." Kissing my man on his lips, we

headed out to the movies. This year, we decided to keep

it simple. We were just happy to be together, and that's

all that mattered. We had it all, and there was nothing

else that could possibly be given. Dinner and a movie it

was. Then back home to mind blowing sex.

My husband was the love of my life, and no bitch

was going to come in between that.

"I love you Kira, and I always will."

"And I'll always love you back."

?

FALLING FOR MY

VALENTINE

☐

REASON NUMBER 10

"I ain't a doctor can't save a life, to say I could I'd be out of my mind. No pro athlete, can't run for miles, that's another thing I won't even try. See there's a lot of things that I can't do, and yea mistakes I make a lot of. There's a couple categories I do, blow the competition out of the water." Like I do- R. Kelly

ZARIA...

This little boy was getting on my damn nerves. When I tell you this lil boy was bad as hell, I don't know what I was thinking. Even though Phantom wasn't hearing voices, his ass was still crazy. The shit had to be genetic because Lil Darryl was straight certified. I've heard of the terrible twos, but this was some other shit.

He defied and went against anything I told him. The only mother fucker he listened to was his daddy, and Freedom. It's like his ass had something against women. He was just mean as fuck.

You would think he was a mama's boy, because he looked just like me. The nigga was my twin, and that was it. We had nothing in common, and he didn't fuck with me at all. Phantom thought the shit was cute, but I was ready to beat his lil ass every chance I got.

"Lil Darryl, come on so you can take a bath. You got food all over you, I need to clean you up." This nigga looked at me with death in his eyes.

"NO."

"What did I say lil boy? Get in here and take this bath."

"I say no. Leave me lone." Grabbing his ass by his arm, this nigga snatched away and stretched his arms. I hated that Phantom taught him that shit, because he knew exactly when to do it. His bad ass started walking towards me, and he had me fucked up. Grabbing my heels, I raised my arms.

"What you saying lil nigga? You don't want these problems. Ask your daddy. Now you can get your ass in the tub, or get knocked out like your pops used to." His ass actually kept his arms up, and stared me down. We were in a full fledge stand off, when Phantom walked in the door.

"What the fuck are yall doing? Are you really about to go to war with your son? Come here lil man, what's wrong." Rolling my eyes, I let his ass deal with

the shit.

"Mean mommy." Phantom actually looked at me

like I was in the wrong.

"I told him to get in the tub, so he could get

cleaned up. He told me no and stretched his arms. You

better get your son." Phantom laughed, and took the

dirty ass lil boy to go wash his ass. "You need to get in

there with him. Your white is not so white anymore."

Looking down at his clothes, he saw the blood splatter

on his shit.

"Good looking out babe. When I'm done with

baby Jesus, imma come kill that pussy. You too damn

uptight. Zee bae need this dick, and she gone get it."

This nigga was patronizing me, and I didn't like the shit.

Raising my shoe, he laughed and walked out. His ass was right though. Lil Darryl been cock blocking for the past two weeks. Every time we get ready to have sex, this nigga would show up out of nowhere. A bitch need some dick shit.

Slamming the pots around, I decided to make my family some dinner. Even though right now I wouldn't mind swiping their shit across the floor, and feeding it to them. I knew they would be hungry in a minute. I should dress the spawn of Satan in all black just to piss they ass off.

Phantom wanted his son to wear nothing but white. Every day, no matter what, Lil Darryl was in white. His ass was too bad to wear white all the damn time. I think he deliberately got food on it. I tried to explain to Phantom that white was not a color for kids. His ass got mad, talking about we got enough money to keep buying more.

They ass was extra, and it was driving me crazy. You would think after two years, I would be used to the shit, but nope. Every day I was ready to pull my hair out. The only exciting thing in my life right now, was Valentine's Day. It was a few weeks away, and I needed a getaway. Since we haven't gotten married yet, I have yet to go out of the country. I bought us tickets to go to Paris, and I couldn't wait.

I haven't told his ass yet, because he acts like he can't pull away from the business to go anywhere. Once he came home, he completely took over as the head nigga in charge, and I paid for it with time. His ass always had something to handle, and it didn't matter what time

of night it was. This lifestyle was stressful, but I knew

what I was getting myself into.

I'm just not as happy as I thought I would be.

Don't get me wrong, I love Phantom with every part of

me. We were happy in love, but I was bored out of my

mind. I hadn't been back to work, and all I do is stay

here and cater to them. I don't mind that, but I need

something else to do with my time.

These past couple of weeks, I barely see Phantom.

He leaves early in the morning, and come home late as

hell. When he walks in the door, I'm sleep and snoring. If

I do stay woke and try to have sex with my man, Lil

Darryl comes in and shut all that shit down. I just wanted

to have something to do. Valentine's Day was that day,

and my ass couldn't wait.

FREEDOM...

I don't know what the hell Phantom was thinking

keeping this shit from Zee. He knew her ass was one visit

away from being crazy just like his ass. Got my ass out all

times of the night and shit with him. Laci been side eying

the fuck out my ass, and I was over this shit. Because her

and Zee were cool now, I couldn't tell her what was

going on. Luckily, the shit was damn near over.

On tomorrow, all the sneaking and shit was gone

be behind us. If me and my girl would last that long. She

didn't trust a nigga as far as she could throw him. Even

though I done proved her ass wrong many times before.

The shit was draining at times, but I knew she was right

to feel like I was up to something this time. Our ass

barely been home, and my ass was tired.

"Free, we gotta go to the warehouse tonight to

make sure everything good. Ain't no telling how long it's

gone be before we get up out of there."

"Nigga, my wife ready to divorce my ass. She at

home with three damn kids, and I'm never there. You

can't do the shit by yourself. We did everything you

could think of."

"Let me find out your bitch got you scared. She

beating on you? I heard yellow niggas be victims and

shit."

"Phantom, straight up. Your ass a half a shade darker than me. Your ass damn near yellow too. Bruh, I'm tired shit. We been at this shit for two weeks. If it ain't right, it ain't never gone be right. My damn feet killing me like I work a damn job." His ass started laughing.

"My bad sus, I didn't know I was fucking up your pedicure. I'll pay to get your feet redone. Your hair too, them curls dryer than my balls. That nigga Lil Darryl don't want me to get no pussy. Yall gone have to baby sit, and let a nigga get some tomorrow." He had me fucked up.

"That nigga don't like Laci, and she be scared to go to sleep when he there. Now your ass trying to stop me from getting some pussy."

"All you have to do is keep him around you. Yall will be straight. Once he go to sleep, wrap your hair up in your bonnet and go get dicked down." I hate this nigga. He was always trying to crack a joke.

"Fuck you bitch. Nigga been out the nut house two days, now he judging and shit. Don't make me grab some LSD. Have you and the voices in that bitch tomorrow. Issa loony. Issa head banger. Issa jello cup." Me and my brother could play like that, and it felt good to be able to laugh like this.

"Fuck you bitch. Just for that, we not going home tonight. I hope she beat your ass until they put you in the field."

"Once upon a time not long ago it was a knot. Bitch Zee stay beating your ass. Let's go check this shit out, so we can go the fuck home. You do the most with your extra ass."

"At least I'm not extra greasy bitch. It's 2018, and your ass still in a jherri curl. Drippy head ass." We headed to the warehouse to make sure his girly ass date was gone be good. If I didn't get no pussy tonight, I was beating his ass.

After making sure everything was good, he dropped me off to my crib and I was happy as hell it didn't take all night. The decorations and everything was perfect. His ass was off his rocker for the date he had set up, but it was cute. She was gone love that shit, cus she was just as crazy as that nigga.

Walking in the door, Laci was standing there looking like a sad lost puppy. I knew it was gone be some bullshit, but I really wasn't out there doing shit. I needed the shit to be kept a secret one more day. On tomorrow, everything would make sense.

"I know that I have put up with a lot of stuff since we been together, and maybe that is the reason you take the shit for granted. I'm sorry if I led you on to believe that I would let you walk over me, but if you think for one second, your ass about to start coming in when you want. You got me fucked up. We are a fucking family, with three kids. I don't care if you were El Chapo, your ass need to find time to bring your ass home.

These past two weeks, your ass have been gone so much, I forget you live here. Now whoever the bitch is, you better tell that hoe the shit is over. You don't want me to fight for my love, cus I will lay your ass out.

Now try me." Not wanting to get into it, I tried to walk

past her. Making a mistake, I bumped her and her ass

went the fuck off again.

"Push a bitch again. PUSH A BITCH AGAIN. Now

you trying to beat a bitch because your lil dick ass out

here cheating." That was my breaking point. Snatching

her ass up, I slammed her down on the table. Snatching

her shorts off, I forced my dick inside her.

"I'm not about to give you no pussy, and you done

fucked the next bitch." She tried to get up, but I

slammed her down again.

"Open your fucking legs before I open them for

you." Spreading her legs for me, I dug deep in her guts. I

knew it wouldn't be long before she started moaning

like crazy. Hitting her spot, I pushed her legs all the way

back. "Squirt on daddy dick." Making sure I stayed on her spot, I worked the fuck out my dick on that mother fucker.

"Oh shit Free, I'm about to cum. Don't stop baby. Right there. You know where to go. Ooh shit."

"Laci shut the fuck up, and squirt on this dick like I told you." Leaning down, I bit her nipple as I rammed my dick into her cervix. Thirty seconds later, her juices were squirting everywhere. Letting my nut ride, I got up to go shower. "Now clean this shit up, so our kids ain't eating their breakfast on our nut."

LACI...

That nigga thought some good dick was gone make me forget his ass was out here cheating. Let's be clear, it was some very good dick. That nigga knew how to put it down, and that was half the reason my ass was going crazy. I wish he would fuck another bitch, all they ass was gone come up missing.

He thought he was about to go to sleep, but I had another trick for his ass. Grabbing a pot out of the kitchen, I filled it up with cold water. Adding some ice to it, I walked up to our bedroom. Pouring all the water and ice on him, I threw the pot at his head for affect.

"Laci what the fuck is wrong with your ass? Don't make me get up and beat your ass. Ignorant ass."

"You think I was letting the shit go that easy? WHO THE FUCK IS THE BITCH THAT YOU ARE SLEEPING WITH. JUST TELL ME WHO SHE IS, SO I CAN GO BEAT HER ASS." Free looked at me like I had lost my mind.

"Laci, I am not cheating on you. Me and Phantom been handling some shit. Yesterday was the last day, now you got me to yourself. Chill the fuck out. Your ass better not be pregnant again. Our baby might fuck around and come out like Lil Darryl."

"Your ass always trying to use Phantom as an excuse to get out of some shit. Own up to your own shit, and just tell me who the fuck it is."

"Call Zee and ask her. I'm sure she will tell you Phantom ass ain't been there either. Now calm your ass down, and clean this fucking water up."

"You think I'm not gone call, but I am. Let her ass act like she don't know what you're talking about. I'm gone fuck you up, and I'm leaving your pretty ass. How the fuck are you prettier than me?" Storming off, I went downstairs to grab my phone. When niggas say call and ask, they be bluffing. They think you will back out of calling, not my ass. Grabbing my phone, I dialed Zee number.

"Mmmm yeah, what's up girl." She sounded busy, but I needed to know what the fuck was up with my man.

"I have a question, has Phantom been gone a lot for the past two weeks? Like not coming home and shit, you barely seeing him?"

"Girl yeah. They had ummmm some kind of business to handle, and they been doing these crazy FUCK hours." What the hell was going on with her ass.

"It's not strange to you that this shit been happening the last two weeks? How do you trust that what he is saying is true?" It took her a few moments to answer me.

"Look, you know who we decided to be with. That's the life they live, and it's the life we chose. Dammmnnn. Now you gone have to put your big girl panties on, and stand by your man." Knowing what she said was true, but the only nigga I had to compare Free to, was Telly. That nigga wasn't shit, but that's the only man I've been with before Free.

My trust issues were a little fucked up, but your man staying out all night was kind of a sign saying he was up to no good. How do you just trust his word that shit is good? Especially when they haven't done the shit before.

"Zaria, how do you trust him so easily."

"Ummm because. He knows I'm crazy. Fuck."

Looking at the phone, I had to know what the hell was

going on with her.

"What the hell is wrong with you? Is Lil Darryl over

there beating your ass?"

"Naw, big Darryl is beating up these guts. I'm gone

call your ass back. This nigga tearing a lining out my ass.

Fuuuuckkkk."

"Bye you nasty bitch." Hanging up the phone, I

had the dumbest look on my face. My man tried to put it

down for me last night, but instead of appreciating it,

and sucking his dick this morning. I woke his ass up to a

pot to the head.

No matter how many times, I fuck up and accused

him of something, I ended up tucking my tail. I don't

know why it was so hard for me to just accept I had a

damn good man. Heading upstairs, I knew I had to

apologize to him.

My ass needed to get my act together before I lost

my man. He was sitting on the bed, waiting on me to

walk through the door. The look on his face let me know

I needed to get my shit together. The last thing I wanted

was for my marriage to be over. Free was my everything,

and I couldn't lose him.

Knowing I needed to break the silence, I hated to

admit I was wrong again. I've done this to him so many

times, I know his ass had to be tired of the shit. The look

on his face, said as much. I'm going to do better. No

matter what, I was gone learn to trust my man.

"Quit looking stupid. I'm not going nowhere, I know you're sorry, now get the fuck over here and suck this dick. You know how I like it too. Sloppy, wet, and deep." Knowing my ass was wrong, I ran to the bed to deep throat my man.

PHANTOM...

Freedom was ready to kill me, and I couldn't do shit but laugh. His ass was in trouble, and it was all my fault. A nigga knew it was gone be some shit behind our disappearances, but it was going to be worth it.

I couldn't do the shit by myself, so Free ass had to get in trouble with me. My girl was just more understanding. She knew I was low key scared of her ass, and that damn bloody shoe. Even if I wasn't a nigga

had everything he wanted at home, and I wouldn't

jeopardize that shit for nobody.

The only problem in our house was my son. I

always laugh, but the shit is almost scary. That nigga is

mean and scary as hell. He stays threatening his mama

and he barely could talk. I've been having talks with him

trying to get him to show her some slack, but his ass

wasn't going. I know my baby was stressing, and tired of

being in here getting threatened by a two-year-old, so I

was putting his ass in daycare. Let his ass threaten

another mother fucker.

It was time for us to leave out, in true fashion, we

were dressed in all white. My baby was looking sexy as

fuck in her white fitted dress, and gold heels. I had on

white jeans, jacket, with white and gold gym shoes. Wrapping a white scarf around my head, it was time to set this shit off.

Jumping in my all white Audi, we headed to the warehouse. When we pulled up, her ass was nervous as fuck. She knew this was where we took niggas we were trying to make disappear, and you could tell she thought her ass was next. Laughing to myself, I got out and opened her door. She actually tried to stall.

"Girl if you don't get your ass out the car, and come on. It's cold as shit out here." Giving me a fake smile, she climbed out. Taking her hand, I led her to the door. Tying a scarf around her eyes, I led her inside. Once I had her all the way in, I untied the scarf and waited for the magic to happen.

"Omg Phantom. This is the most beautiful thing ever." With tears in her eyes, she ran and jumped in my arms. I had the warehouse decorated like Elgin the psych hospital where we met. My office mirrored hers, we were standing in the dayroom, and I had another room made like mine.

"This symbolizes the place I fell in love at first sight. You changed my world in so many ways, and I needed you to understand you changed my life. If it wasn't for you, a nigga wouldn't even be free." Leading her to a table in the dayroom, I pulled her chair out and sat her down.

Our food was even catered on the hospital trays. I went all out to recreate the shit. The first thing she brought me to eat was a beef from Portillos, and that was what we were having today. As we ate our beef

sandwiches, her ass sat there crying. I knew she was

going to be happy, but I wasn't done yet. Taking her

hand, I led her to her office. On her desk, it was a

jewelry case full of rings sitting there.

"Two years ago, I asked you to marry me. I did it in

the spur of the moment, but I meant every word I said.

Knowing you deserve the best, here I stand asking you

again. I refuse to go another year and you're not my

wife. I know shit been hard lately, but I promise after

today, you will never be unhappy again.

Every day, I want to find a different reason to

make you smile. As long as I'm living, I will give you the

world two times over. You've given me everything, and

I'm begging you to let me give it back. Zaria will you

marry me, on Valentine's Day?"

"Yes, baby. Yes." Kissing her, I walked her over to

the jewelry case.

"Pick any ring you want." Of course, her ass

grabbed the biggest one out of the case. Ten carats,

clear, princess cut. Sliding it on her finger, I kissed her

again. Grabbing her hand, the surprise wasn't over.

Getting back in the car, I drove her to the next spot.

An office building downtown. Using my key, I

walked her inside. She was looking confused, and I knew

she didn't understand what was going on.

"This is your office. You have your own practice,

and I'm putting Lil Darryl in daycare. You get to go back

to doing what you love. Without having to work for someone else."

"You are the fucking best nigga in the world, and all I had to do was beat your ass with a shoe. Who would have thought. I wonder what I could get if I hit your ass with a bat."

"Shut the fuck up, and come suck this dick. I'm feeling kind of crazy with and them voices might be coming back." Laughing, she walked over to me and unzipped my pants. This was about to be the best head a nigga got.

⸮

REASON NUMBER ELEVEN

"There is only one for me, you have made that a possibility. We can take that step to see, if this is really gonna be. All you gotta do is say yes. Don't deny what you feel let me undress you baby, open up your mind just rest. I'm about to let you know you make me so so so so so so so so." Say Yes- Floetry

LACI...

This wedding was driving everybody crazy. Who in the hell decides to get married in two damn weeks. Of course, I was the maid of honor, so I had to help her do all this shit.

She didn't have an idea of where she wanted to have the wedding, a caterer, venue for the reception. We need to go dress shopping, and everything else. Not to mention, her ass ain't got no friends. None of us do. The wedding was going to consist of us four, and his damn workers.

It was crazy how none of us were connected to our families, but we had each other. I guess that's why we got along so well. It was just us against the world. Maybe the workers could bring their girls, and it would at least fill up some of the space, so we wouldn't look pathetic.

Jumping in my car, I headed over to Zee's house. We needed to get on the ball, and I hated working under pressure. This was definitely pressure, I was going crazy and it wasn't even my wedding. When I pulled up, Zee was running out the door. She jumped in the car, and you would think Phantom was about to beat her ass.

"What the hell is wrong with you? Phantom about to get in that ass. You weren't running fast enough though. That nigga like Michael Myers, he will catch your ass doing his slow walk."

"Something like that. That mother fucking demon child of mine was trying to get me. I promise if Phantom wasn't there at night, I wouldn't go to sleep with his ass there. His ass is crazy." I could not stop laughing. She was really scared of her two-year-old son. I'm not gone lie, I was scared of his ass too, but I wasn't his mama.

"Zee, it cannot be that bad. What he do?"

"The nigga just chased me to the door, arms stretched, holding a butter knife. All because I told his ass I couldn't make his sandwich, Phantom would. I'm telling you, that nigga wants to kill me."

"Girl you better whoop that demon child. Don't make no sense you scared of your own damn baby." Driving to the bridal shop, we went to pick out our dresses.

I picked mine out from the start. I fell in love with an off the shoulder periwinkle silk gown. The shit hugged my body like fucking glove. Zee on the other hand, we were on dress ten, and she still wasn't happy. Even though I was ready to go, I haven't saw one that screamed this is the one either.

When she walked out this time, I knew the wait was over. This dress hugged her body, and cuffed under her ass. The rest of it flared out, and flowed in a train. The shit was sexy as fuck. The top had some stones on it that looked like diamonds, and it looked perfect on her. When I saw the tears in her eyes, I knew she agreed with me.

"Laci, I'm glad you're with me to share this moment. Times like this, you wish you had your mom around, but at least I got somebody. This is the one, I want it."

"I wouldn't want to be anywhere else. Now hurry up and pay that twenty k, so we could get the hell out of here. I'm hungry as hell. Only you would take five hours to find a dress."

"Girl shut up, you can't rush beauty. I am hungry as shit though. Maybe I should have made that damn sandwich." We both laughed as she went to take the dress off. This Valentine's Day was going to be special as hell, and I knew it would be a day she would never forget.

Once we were done in the dress shop, we took our ass to Grand Luxe. I couldn't wait to get some chicken wraps. As we sat there waiting on the waitress, I couldn't help but think how happy she was about to be walking down that aisle.

Me and Free went to the courthouse, because we had nobody to be there. Every girl dreams about having a big wedding. All I got was a piece of paper, and three kids. On our anniversary, I was gone talk to Free about renewing our vows. My ass was gone get my day to walk

down the aisle, and feel like every girl should. I was

happy as hell for Zee, and that gave me new found

energy to finish the rest of our day. No matter what, we

were going to get everything handled, and she would

have the best wedding ever.

PHANTOM...

"Why the hell do girls make a big deal out of a

fucking wedding. We could have done this shit in our big

ass house, and kicked it after. We don't even know

anybody. Who the hell is on that guest list?" Freedom

was here with me, since it was the night before my

wedding. Zee was there with Laci. I had to keep Lil Darryl

with me, because he was bound to kill Zee ass in her

sleep.

"She got the workers as guests and that's it. You

know our dysfunctional asses don't fuck with nobody,

but each other."

"Call they ass, tell them to bring they girls with

them. My baby wants a big wedding, and dammit she

gone have one. Anybody who owes me money, make

they asses come too." Freedom laughed at me, but I was

dead ass serious. I was Phantom, there was no way I was

gone have a sad ass wedding.

"You sure you don't want to have a bachelor

party? We supposed to go all the way out, and we sitting

in the house like some old ass niggas." Thinking about

how the hood would be talking shit, I knew I couldn't go out like that.

"Call the niggas. Tell they ass to come over. Bring food, liquor, and bitches. They not about to tell the hood Phantom ass an old ass nigga. We about to do this shit up. If it's boring, I'm stretching my arms on you niggas. Oh, tell them their asses gotta wear all white."

"Aww shit, it's about to go down in this mother fucker. You better make sure Zee don't find out, or your ass gone be at your wedding knotted up. Dizzy than a mother fucker. You can't go to your wedding as a victim."

"Nigga, just make the call damn. Your ass talks too damn much. I'm not about to fuck one of the bitches, we just gone party." I'm sure Zee was gone be mad that I had a party at the house, but a nigga wasn't going out

like willie lump lump.

"Hey, who is Willie lump lump?" Free looked at

me like I was crazy.

"Nigga I don't know. Where the fuck that shit

come from? Far as I know, your ass Willie lump lump.

You the one getting hit with shoes and shit."

"Fuck you bitch. Let me go get ready, nigga go find

you some white." Free left, and it was time to go out

with a bang.

****

The bachelor party was a success, and I was glad

that we had it. Me and Free sat back and watched these

bitches shake that ass. We partied like it was my last

time, and it kind of gave a nigga second thoughts. I was about to be missing out on all this free pussy, and the shit was thrown at me left and right. I know there was no other bitch out there for me, but damn. I never thought I would see the day Phantom would settle down.

Shaking those thoughts off, I grabbed me and lil man shit and headed to the church. No bitch out here was better than Zee bae, and if I tried to back out, she would beat my ass anyway. That's what I loved most about her ass. She got me, and that was all that mattered to me.

Most women, the wedding is strictly about them. I told Zee that I wanted our shit to be different and I convinced her to stand at the front and wait for me. I was an extra ass nigga, and I wanted to walk in while everybody watched me come down the aisle. Why the chick had to be the one making an entrance. I'm the dramatic one in the relationship, so it was only right.

She laughed at my ass, and agreed. The guests were going to be shocked, but who gave a fuck what they thought. I'm that nigga, and I'll kill all they ass. It was about me and Zee, and we were gone do the shit how we wanted to do it.

"Come on Lil man. Daddy has to go marry the woman of his dreams. Do you remember what we practiced?"

"Yes daddy."

"Okay good." I kind of didn't mention this part to Zee, she wouldn't have agreed if she knew I was gone be this damn extra. Me and my son was about to steal the

show. Driving to the hall, we headed to our room to get

dressed. Making sure they had our walking music, I

smiled at the shock that was going to cross Zee face.

Fuck that, it's my wedding too. I was about to send this

shit up. Don't nobody want to be at no boring ass

wedding.

Me and my Lil man dressed in our all white as

normal. I tied a scarf around his head, and then did

mine. Looking at him, I couldn't be prouder. He looked

like his mom, but he was me through and through.

"It's time nigga let's go." Freedom was my best

man, so he walked down the aisle first. After he was

there, me and Lil man stood at the doors. Waiting on my

song to play, I laughed. The doors swung open as the

intro played. It would be the only time they could hear me. Me and Lil man stretched our arms wide, and walked in the door.

"Yea thou I walk through the valley and the shadow of death, I will fear no evil for thou art with me." Everybody looked at us in shock trying to figure out what was going on. Usually when I do my calling card, that meant I was about to kill somebody. Not today, I just wanted to come in as me. My music started, and we kept our arms stretched.

"I'm strapped up nigga fuck a gun law. See me walking with a limp, that's my gun walk. I don't do no arguing I let the gun talk." I knew Zee was going to be shocked, but I didn't expect the look that she gave me. Before I could say anything, she took off running from the front. When I say her ass took off running, her ass

took the fuck off. I don't know how she moved that fast

in a wedding dress, but Zee was gone. The mother

fucker was jumping benches and everything trying to get

the fuck out of there.

Everybody tried to look to me for answers, but I

didn't have a clue what the fuck was going on. I blinked,

and Zee ass was ghost. Freedom walked up to me,

looking for an explanation.

"What the fuck wrong with your girl? She ran up

out of here like a running back. How the fuck she jump

them seats with them heels on?"

"I don't' know, I'm about to go find her. Don't let

anybody leave. If they get up shoot they ass. I'm coming

back with my bride. I'll be damned if Phantom get stood

the fuck up."

"Do I gotta keep Lil Darryl too?"

"Yeah nigga. Your ass scared of a two-year-old

too?" We laughed, and I ran out of the hall. A nigga ain't

see shit but smoke and skid marks from her heels.

LACI...

"Free, what in the fuck just happened? I'm lost as

hell. Why would Phantom try to kill Zee? What did she

do?" I was scared as hell, and I didn't know what the

fuck to do. Should I be running, and getting the fuck out

of dodge as well?

"Phantom is handling it, and no he wasn't trying to kill her. Why would you think that?" Were we at the same damn wedding?

"Because he stretched his damn arms, and said the scripture. My ass was ready to duck and hide. I'm just trying to figure out why the hell he trying to kill her." You could see the thoughts running through his head. Then he started laughing hard as hell.

"She must have thought the same thing, and that's why her ass ran out of here. That is funny as hell. He was just as clueless as us, and we have no idea where she went." Okay, if both of them were gone, why in the hell were we still here.

"We can leave then right? He has no idea where she is, and it seems to me the wedding is off. Then why are we sitting our dumb ass here looking stupid?"

"Phantom said if anyone leaves, kill them. Unless your ass ready to cross over, you better sit your ass down and make sure no one else walks up out of here."

That was some straight up bullshit. If she ran up out of here, and he don't know where she is, how was there going to be a wedding? We were sitting here for nothing, and the shit wasn't fair. This dress was hot as hell, and I wanted to be away from their crazy asses.

Trying to sneak away, I eased out the side door and walked to the back room. When I'm nervous, I have to eat. There was no food in the hall we were in, but it was snacks and stuff in the room where she got dressed.

As I went down the hall, I heard a gun cock back. This nigga had lost his mind, and I was ready to beat his ass. Turning around, Free was standing there with a gun pointed at me.

"This is going to be the last time you pull a gun on me for Phantom. Put that shit away before I beat your ass." The nigga laughed, and put the gun away.

"I need some action, and I was hoping your ass was about to make a run for it. Now that I see the direction you're running in, I know your fat ass trying to go get some food. Damn shame, we in a crisis and your ass thinking about food. Go sit your hungry ass down."

"Don't judge me nigga. You know when my nerves bad I eat a lot. Shit. They ass not here no way. Give a bitch a biscuit or something."

"Fuck a biscuit, you can eat this dick though." No matter what goes on, this nigga was thinking about some pussy. If they didn't hurry up and figure this shit out soon, I was gone be in the back eating dick and doughnuts. It's Valentine's Day and my ass stuck in a hall just looking stupid.

ZARIA...

When that nigga came through the doors of that hall, my heart damn near fell out of my chest. The only thing that went through my mind is why the fuck was this nigga trying to kill me? We hadn't gotten into it or nothing. It was no reason for his retarded ass to pull this shit. Not to mention, he had my son in on the shit. The

damn seed of chucky might have been the one to

convince him to do it. Tricked both they ass. I started to

yell out, sike yo mind yo booty shine. A bitch was

running a full marathon. I didn't even catch a cab, that's

how scared a bitch was. I ran all the way to the house.

By the time I made it in, I was two seconds away

from passing out. What in the fuck was I thinking? After I

got far enough away, I should have jumped my ass in an

Uber or something. I bet my ass looked bout dumb as

hell running through the streets of Chicago in a wedding

dress.

As soon as I made it in my house, I grabbed my

luggage and threw what I could in there. I knew I didn't

have long before he came looking for me, and my ass

was gone be on that midnight train to Georgia. You may

as well call me Gladys Knight. Matter fact, they can call a

bitch the Pips. Either way, my ass was gone. Going in the

safe I grabbed some cash, and I was ready to go. I would

change my clothes once I made it the fuck away from

here.

The tears welled up in my eyes, and I just didn't

understand. Who in the fuck tries to kill somebody on

their wedding day? This was the worst Valentine's Day

ever. Fuck him. Turning around out the closet, I was out

this bitch. Or so I thought. His ass was standing behind

me.

"Please just let me leave. You don't have to want

me, that's fine. Just please don't kill me. WHY THE FUCK

WOULD YOU WANT TO KILL ME. I HATE YOU SO MUCH

RIGHT NOW. I don't hate you, please don't kill me. I'm your child's mother." The nigga didn't say shit, and it pissed me off. "Try it if you want to, we gone be some dead mother fuckers in this bitch. What you wanna do? Come on nigga, because you got me fucked up." He laughed so hard he had tears running down his face.

"Zee. Why the hell would I want to kill you? I'm so fucking lost right now. One minute I'm about to marry the love of my life, the next all I see is ass, feet, and elbows. Come here. What's going on?" Was this nigga trying to trick me? Walking to him cautiously, I fell into his embrace.

"When you walked in the doors, you had your arms stretched and you said the scripture. Everybody knows what that mean. I was not about to stay and

catch a fade on my wedding day."

"Zee bae. Daddy was being extra. I just wanted to

come in on my wedding like only I could. I didn't think

your ass was gone take it as me doing my calling card.

Before I could explain, your ass was gone with the wind.

I ain't even know your ass could move that damn fast.

You ran the heel off them bitches." We both laughed our

asses off. "Now can we go get married now?"

"How? I'm sure everyone is gone by now. I fucked

up my damn wedding day. I'm sorry." Trying my best not

to cry, the tears found their way down my face.

"Everyone is still there. I told Free if anyone tried

to leave, kill them." When he didn't crack a smile, I knew

he was dead ass serious. Using his thumb to wipe my tears, he leaned down and kissed me.

"Come on, it's time for me to become Mrs. Reed. I'm ready, and I promise I won't run this time."

"You better not, or I will shoot you in the ass. Let's go, I should push your ass down the stairs trying to leave me at the altar. I'm mother fucking Phantom. You can't do this shit to me." Laughing, he scooped me up and carried me down the stairs. I couldn't wait to say I do.

"When we get to the hall, can we just walk down the aisle together?" Nodding his head while he laughed at my expense, I calmed down a little. A bitch was gone side eye him until we said I do.

Phantom texted Free and let him know we were about to walk in, and have everyone seated. Giving them a little time, we wanted to make sure everyone was ready. I made him text Free a new song to play for us to walk to. Looking at him, I knew I could be with this man forever. As long as he never tries to kill me. Kissing him, the doors opened while we were in our embrace.

"When I'm with you I wonder why, people do stop and stare and smile at us. When I'm with you, the sun shines my way. Baby our love reflects its rays of light, on everyone in the world when I'm with you. It's for real. What I feel, when I'm with you."

Hand in hand, we walked down the aisle. Tears fell down my face again, but this time it was from pure happiness and love. This man had given so much, and all I could do was cry. I loved him with my entire being, and I knew he felt the same. Tears fell down his face as well, and that took away any doubt. This was where I was

supposed to be, and I didn't want to be anywhere else.

We saved each other, and he was all the fuck I needed.

We got to the front, and my bad ass son was standing

there giving me death looks. I wanted to flick his bad ass

off, but I couldn't. That was my son. Grabbing his hand, I

pulled him to the front with us. This was my family. Take

us as we were. The Reeds.

MY SAVAGE

VALENTINE

REASON NUMBER TWELVE

"Tell me it's real, the feeling that we feel. Tell me that it's real. Don't love come just past us by, try. It's all we have to do, it's up to me and you. To make it this special love last forever more." Tell Me It's Real- KCI & JOJO

MODEST...

Leaving out of the office, a nigga was beat. This legal life was worse than the street shit. In the streets, I didn't have to think, or second guess. I knew that shit in my sleep, this shit took effort. All the shit was worth it though when I saw the smile on my baby's face. Me and

Malae was going strong, and a nigga never been happier. Who would have ever thought that a love like this, would have come from a lil boy begging at the gas station.

Tyler gave me so much life, and a nigga loved how he saw me as his father. Even though me and Malae ended up having a daughter of our own, Ty was my first love. His ass let me know that I could be a great father. I never even thought about being a dad, until him. Malae was due any day now, and I couldn't wait until our baby girl got here.

We decided to name her Malia, and I knew she was gone have me wrapped around her finger. Malae ran me ragged, and I did that shit with a smile. Not once ever complaining. I don't understand how any nigga could be a deadbeat. The shit was exciting, and I

couldn't wait until my baby came. She was gone have

the world, and not naan mother fucker better mess with

her. After I stopped at the store and got Malae some ice

cream, I headed in the house. She was sitting on the

couch looking like a can of busted biscuits. Her shit was

seeping through the seams of everything.

I didn't even know an ankle, and a foot could swell

up that big. You could tell she was in pain. Grabbing her

leg, I laid them across mine and started massaging them.

Her ass literally started moaning.

"Baby, it's almost over. Keep that in mind, and

remember your man is right here. I got you ma, don't

you forget that. I'm about to go run you a bath." Passing

her the ice cream, I went upstairs and drew her a bath.

This pregnancy was getting the best of her, but I needed her to know that I was here. Once the water was ready, I headed downstairs and her ass was sleep with the spoon in her mouth. Putting her ice cream up, I picked her up and carried her upstairs. Laying her in the bed, I undressed her.

Even though she was sleep, I massaged her body hoping it will make her feel better. I've never seen somebody snore and moan at the same time. Covering her up, I headed to Ty's room to check on him. Like always, his ass was playing the game.

"Hey daddy. You wanna play the game with me? I'm tired of beating the computer." His ass never even looked up at me.

"You couldn't beat me on your good day. It's time to go to bed son. We can play tomorrow. Go take your bath, and lay it down."

"Five more minutes daddy, please." Not knowing how to say no to him, I agreed to five more minutes. Leaving him to play in peace, I headed downstairs to my home office. Looking at our security cameras, I looked at the car that had been parking outside every day for the last four days. I saw the same car on the office security camera.

The crazy part about it was, I never caught the mother fucker out there. When I check the tapes, it would be there. Someone was watching me, and I had no idea who. Not wanting to send Malae into a panic, or my brother back into street mode, I decided to give it a minute before I reacted. They could be creeping with

one of the neighbors, or visiting them. I told myself it

was my mind missing the streets, but in my heart, I knew

it was something else. Time would tell, and if they were

on some bullshit, they was getting that wig shifted sixty

degrees north.

"Baby, where are you?" Malae was woke and

looking for my ass. Shutting the tapes off, I walked up

the stairs to find my girl.

"I'm right here. What's wrong ma? You need me

to go get something? You good?"

"I'm okay, just woke up and you weren't there.

Something just feels off, what are you doing?" Not

wanting to tell her about the car, I left it alone.

"Nothing at all ma, let's go to bed. You need something from down here?" When she shook her head no, I turned off everything. Checking in on Ty, he was already sleep and in bed. The house was peaceful, and I was about to lay down with my girl. I would protect her no matter what, just hope I didn't have to break my promise to her. My savage needed to stay buried.

AKINA….

Sitting here staring at this test, I was still in shock. I couldn't believe I was pregnant. It's not like me and Meek were being careful, but I don't know if I could deal with this. The minute the test read pregnant, I thought about Gabbie. How could I ever bring myself to have another baby, when I blamed myself for her death? My

ass would be scared to do anything, ignore her, or even

tell her no. My ass would be a nervous wreck, and I

don't think I'm ready for that.

What if something happened to this baby? There

is no way I could survive that. I barely survived Gabbie.

Had it not been for Meek, I would be just a shell of a

woman. Wrapping the test in tissue, I hid it at the

bottom of the trash can. There was no way Meek would

understand me being scared to have this baby.

His ass love kids. Him and Modest practically be

fighting over Ty, and all he talks about is when his niece

gets here. I wouldn't tell him until I knew for sure or not

I was going to keep this baby. This was the worst

decision I ever had to make, but I hated that I had to

make it alone. My mama would be ecstatic, so she would be no help to me. I cut all my friends off when I lost Gabbie because nobody understood what I was going through. Fuck it, me and Malae was cool. She was unbiased, and I think she will give me some good advice. Grabbing my phone, I called her.

"Hey Kina. Where your ass been? Don't make me tell Meek your ass pushing me away. You know he don't play that shit. How you gone neglect your God child? Your ass gotta do better." I felt bad that I hadn't talked to her. I've been trying to avoid anybody because my ass been sick. I didn't want nobody figuring the shit out, until I knew if I was pregnant.

"I'm sorry, but you may have your own God child to neglect. I just took a test, and I'm pregnant."

"Well damn bitch, cue the violin. Your ass sound depressed as hell when you should be happy. Meek gone blow his top when he finds out." My silence must have let her know I wasn't too thrilled.

"You didn't tell him. Ok Kina, what's going on? Why haven't you told Meek, and why do you sound like your ass just got a death sentence."

"I've never told you this, but I had a daughter. I was too busy working, and didn't go check on her when she told me her chest was hurting. When I finally did, she was already dead. I don't think I could ever get past that. How do I have another baby, and I'm living with that kind of guilt?" She sighed, and I could tell she really didn't know how to answer that.

"That's big. I couldn't even imagine how that must feel, but I know you. Kina you will be a great mom. You made a simple mistake, and I know you won't make it again. You have to find a way to move past it. Just go to the doctor, and see how you feel once you hear the heartbeat. It changed my life."

"Thank you. I'll go stop by now. Please don't mention this to Modest. I need to know what I'm going to do first before I break the news."

"Okay boo, but you got this." Hanging up, I grabbed my keys and went to the doctor. My ass was nervous as hell, but Malae was right. The sound of its heartbeat made me feel some type of way, but I don't know if it was big enough for me to decide to keep it.

"Doctor, how far am I, and how long do I have before it's too late to choose other options?"

"You have six weeks to decide. Anything after that, you're putting yourself at risk. It will also be an actual baby, and I don't approve of those kind of terminations. Here is some paperwork. You have a little while to make a decision. When you come back for your next appointment, you can let me know what you are deciding to do."

"Thank you doctor." Heading home, it was so many thoughts running through my mind. Before I knew it, I was at home. Meek was there, and I hid the papers in my purse. As soon as I walked in the door, he was on my ass.

I was not in the mood for sex, but how do I tell him I'm not in the mood. I've never told him no, and if I do now, he will know something was up.

"Baby, take that shit off. I need that pussy. I'm on my lunch break and I need that shit in my mouth right now." His ass was excited, and all I wanted to do was cry.

MALAE...

A year ago, nobody could have told me this would be my life. I was broke, starving, and gang banging. Some days, I didn't know where my next meal was coming from. Now my biggest problem was turning down food. I was big as shit, but my baby always made me feel like I was the sexiest bitch he knew. I appreciated the fact that he went out of his way to boost my ego, but at the end of the day, my ass was big. I didn't even know certain places could stretch. My damn pussy was fat as hell, on top of my ankles. The back of my knees had even grown fat.

My neck was black, and my nose was bigger than my pussy was. I hated when he stared at me, because I was scared he would notice how ugly I was. Instead he would rub me down, and tell me I'm the most beautiful woman he ever seen. The shit felt good, but I hate that he had to lie to me, so I could feel good about myself.

I'm not blind, I know my ass look a hot mess. Standing in the mirror, I looked at me in all my ugliness. I was naked as hell, and I could see it all. Even though I knew it was from the baby, it still brought tears to my eyes.

"Baby what are you doing? Bring your sexy ass over here. Let me see if you taste as good as you look."

"Your ass just eat pussy now huh. I remember when you had to ask me what to do, now look at you." We laughed, and he licked his lips.

"Don't play with me, you know damn well I'm the pussy fucking monster. Now bring your sexy ass over here so I can show you." The smile dropped from my face, and I looked back in the mirror.

"Baby, you don't have to lie to me. I know I look a mess, but I love you so much for trying to make me feel better." His smile faded, and I could tell he was no longer in joking mode.

"Bring your ass here." Walking over to him, I felt like I was in trouble. "Feel this." Placing my hand on his brick hard dick, my pussy jumped. "If I didn't mean what I said, this bitch wouldn't be hitting the floor. You're carrying my child. Everything about that is sexy to me. What you have to go through to give me something priceless, got a nigga on brick all day every fucking day. Let me hear you say that shit again, we gone have a problem. Now you gone let me taste it or what?"

"If you eat it with some ice cream like you did last time." My pussy shuddered from the thought.

"I'll be right back. I'm about to run to the corner store. Your ass better be laid up ready for me too."

He wasn't gone but five minutes when Ty came to the door. Screaming my name.

"Yea baby."

"Daddy is at the door. He said come here." What the fuck. He was supposed to be coming up here to eat this pussy. I been pushing his ass down further on the slick side. I almost got him accidentally eating my ass. I was looking forward to this head. Throwing on a robe, I ran downstairs with an attitude. Why the fuck didn't he use his key anyway. Snatching the door open, I almost passed the fuck out when I saw who was there.

"June what the fuck." This nigga wasn't dead, but alive and well at my front fucking door.

"You look surprised to see me. Especially since you done moved on, and fucking on a new nigga. As if he knew someone was near his pussy, Modest walked in the door. He looked at June, but didn't acknowledge him. Walking the ice cream to the freezer, he put it away and then came back. Walking back to where we were standing, he stood next to me.

"Don't stop talking. We listening." Modest vein was bulging, even though he appeared to be calm.

"You moved on to the nigga that tried to kill me, and left me for dead?"

"But did you die?" Trying not to laugh, I knew I needed to step in. I couldn't believe I was looking at my first love in my face. This man had my soul, and ripped it out when he died. Only, he wasn't dead.

"Where the hell have you been all this time? Do you know what your death did to me and Ty? We struggled, we ached, we barely survived." The tears started to fall, and I could tell Modest felt a certain kind of way.

"My son acted like he didn't give a fuck when he just saw me. It's obvious yall done turned him against me." That got a smirk out of Modest, I'm sure that made him feel good.

"My son don't give a fuck about you. Now if you don't have a reason to be in my house, get the fuck out."

"Or what." This was not how this shit should be going. I'm still trying to process my feelings about seeing June. For as long as I could remember, that man held my heart. All those feelings came flooding back, and I didn't know what to do with them.

I loved Modest, but this shit here, I didn't know what to do. All I know is that in this moment, standing here, I was in love with two men. I would have never

gotten with Modest if June was still alive, and I didn't

know if I still felt the same about June as I did before he

died. This was some messy shit, and before I knew it, my

ass passed out.

MEEK...

Akina and me had been doing so well, I took pride

in the fact that I helped her heal. She needed special

attention, and I had to handle her a certain way. I've

worked long, and hard to help her come to terms with

her daughter's death.

We go to the grave all the time, and she no longer

breaks down. It took some time, but she can talk about

her and look at her picture without crying now. Akina

was now able to speak about her with pride. For

Valentine's Day, I wanted to do something special for

her. I wanted us to dedicate celebrating our special day,

to Gabbie. Everything would be about her. We were

grown, we didn't need Valentine's Day to solidify how

we felt about each other.

As I said, we were in a good place. Until lately.

See, I was the type of nigga that new every part of my

girl's body, and I could tell when something was off.

Every time I wanted to have sex, she would do it, but

you could see it all in her face that she didn't want to. I

was about to get to the bottom of it though.

"Akina, take your fucking pants off." The look on

her face told me I was right about how I was feeling. She

obliged, but she damn sure didn't want to. "Spread your legs." When she did it, I walked over to her and dived my face in her pussy. Licking up her slit nice and slow, I pulled back and made her watch me enjoy her juices.

"Do you think I know the taste of my pussy?" I could tell she didn't know how to answer that, so I continued. "When I eat your pussy, do you think I enjoy and savor every last drop?" Sliding my finger inside her for emphasis, I put it in my mouth nice and slow. Making my way up to her breast, I took her hardened nipple in my mouth. Moans escaped her mouth, even though she wanted to fight it.

"Do you think I know what makes your nipples stand up, and get goosebumps around your areola?" My baby was still stuck, but I still wasn't done. Pulling my dick out, I rubbed it against her clit. "Open your fucking

legs Akina." Spreading them for me, I rubbed my shit up

and down on her clit occasionally dipping my tip inside.

"Do you think I know what to do to get your

muscles to close around my dick? What makes you drip?

How to pull a nut out of you on command. This is my

pussy, my body, I know everything about you. How the

fuck did you think I wouldn't know you were pregnant?"

Jumping up, I could tell she was shocked to shit.

"I'm sorry for not telling you. It's just so much on

my mind about it. You know what I went through, and I

don't want to mess up again." Pushing her down, I slid

my dick back inside her.

"You won't mess up again, because you have me.

On days you need a break because it's something you

needed to do, I would take over. If you just wanted to have a girl's night, I'll get the baby." Making sure I stroked her long and hard, I continued to stress my point. "I would never allow you to get overwhelmed, and I would never let you do everything. I'm that nigga, and you my girl. Don't fucking play with me." No longer talking, I fucked my point across to her. When her body started shaking, I released all inside my walls.

"I'm so glad we had this talk, I've had a headache all day because I was stressing over this shit. Can you go to my purse and get me some Tylenol baby daddy?" Slapping her on her ass, I got up.

"I'm daddy, but not your baby daddy. Don't make me come put this dick back in your life. I'll forget your ass pregnant and flip you all over this fucking house."

Laughing, I ran upstairs to get the pills. I didn't expect to find this shit though. Running back downstairs, it took everything in me not to knock her ass out. Everything I thought I knew about her, went out the fucking window. She was a dirty ass snake just like all the other women out here. Throwing the papers in her face, I waited until she looked at them, so she could understand why I was pissed.

"You were gone kill my baby without even fucking telling me you were pregnant? You got me fucked up." You could tell it was so much she wanted to say, but I didn't want to hear the shit. Right now, all I wanted to do was get the fuck away from her. Just as I was about to lay into her ass before I did a dramatic ass exit, my phone rung. Seeing it was Modest, I picked up.

"Get to the hospital, Malae just passed out and now her ass in labor."

"What the fuck happened? Never mind, I'll find out when I get there. I'm on the way. She's at UIC right."

"Yea, see you in a minute." You could tell Akina was scared to ask me to go, but I wasn't that damn petty. She was the God mama, so she had just as much right to be there as me.

"If you are going with me, quit looking stupid and get your ass up. We have to go." I was still pissed, but we would deal with this after we left the hospital.

?

REASON NUMBER THIRTEEN

"I am in love with you, you set me free baby. I

can't do this thing called life without you here with me.

Cause I'm dangerously in love with you. I'll never leave.

Just keep loving me. The way I love you loving me."

Dangerously In Love- Beyonce

MODEST...

This nigga thought he was gone come back and

disturb what the fuck I built with my family, he had me

fucked up. We had been through too much for his ass to

come waltz his dead ass back in here. When I saw my girl

hit the floor, I was gone make sure his ass was down

there with her. He wanted to be with her, I happily

obliged. Giving his ass an uppercut that shook his soul,

he flew halfway across the room. The nigga shoe was

still by the door. Running upstairs, I grabbed Ty and

headed back downstairs. Kicking the nigga as I passed

him, I scooped my girl up and we were out. Looking

down at the shoe, I couldn't believe my girl was in love

with this nigga and his ass around here wearing

Sketchers. Dirty ass Sketchers.

Once I started driving, I called one of my old

workers. There was no way I was about to leave his ass

in my house. It looks like his ass might try and steal.

"Hey bro, I need you to swing by my house and

pick up a package."

"Is it permanent?"

"Naw, just rocked they ass. Go do that asap. Mother fucker in Sketchers." He laughed, and I knew I didn't have to say anything else.

"On the way now, bro." Hanging up, I drove as fast as I could to UIC. She still hadn't woken up yet, and the shit was scaring me. It seemed like it took me forever, but I finally got there. Me and Ty jumped out, and I carried her inside.

"Can I get some help. My girl nine months pregnant, and she passed out." The nurses rushed over, and took her towards the back. I tried to follow her, but they wouldn't let me.

"Sir, let us see what is going on. Someone will come and give you an update. Let us help her." Sitting down, I was mad at myself for not killing that nigga.

What if she wanted to go back to him? The only reason she was with me, is because she thought he was dead. How in the fuck was his ass still alive anyway? I lit that nigga up, and made sure he took his last breath. That nigga must got Houdini in his blood. Or power ups in his Sketchers.

So much was on my mind, and for the first time in forever, I was scared. For my baby, and for my family. If I lost them, I don't know what the fuck I would do. Ty was mine, and I was willing to kill that nigga. He should have hit that power up before I bonded with the lil nigga.

"Daddy it's going to be okay. Mommy won't leave us. She strong, and drink lots of milk." Hugging my lil man, I forgot I needed to be strong for him. Yet, here he was pulling me up.

"Yes she is, cus she my girl. Our family not weak. She got this." I spoke the words, but I was more worried about her leaving me for that clown ass nigga. They had history, and I was the reason they went through all of that.

"Sir, your girlfriend is in labor. We need you to come back." Jumping up, we ran towards the room. I was not about to miss her having my daughter. Grabbing my phone, I called my brother and told him what was going on. The nurses took Ty to the family room, and I washed up.

This shit had me nervous as hell, but right now, I needed to be here for my girl. My baby looked like shit, but she managed to give me a weak smile. Walking over to her, I grabbed her hand.

"You ready beautiful?" Nodding her head yes, I leaned down and kissed her. Trying to get through the birth, I ignored the fact that she didn't kiss me back. That was a sure sign that I was in trouble, and her ass was about to leave, but I couldn't think about that right now.

The doctor told her when to push, and my baby did the shit like a champ. The occasional tears fell down her face, but I kissed them away and talked her through it. Finally, my baby girl was here.

"Does she have a name?"

"Malia Monet Matthews." Looking into my baby girl's eyes, there was no way I was letting that ugly ass nigga win. If I had to kill his ass again, I would. No matter what, I wasn't letting my family go. Walking out the room to get Ty, I saw Meek and Kina sitting there.

Waving them back, you could tell they ass was going

through it too. I don't know why all the holidays have to

be hard for the Matthew brothers, but this was one L, I

wasn't taking.

We all walked back in the room, and Malae

couldn't even look at me. The shit was breaking my

heart, but her ass was about to grieve all over again. If

she thought I was letting her leave me, to go back to

that nigga she had me fucked up. I ate her pussy, no

other bitch in the world can say that. My ass wasn't

down there sucking on pussy lips, choking on hair and

shit, cus she couldn't shave right with her belly. Pussy

had patches and shit, but I ate that shit like it was soul

glo.

Everybody was going crazy over Malia, until that clown ass nigga walked in the room. Malae's eyes got big, and Meek looked like he had seen a ghost.

"Maybe I wasn't clear when I laid your ass out." Before I could send that nigga on a permanent nap, Malae stopped me.

"Can you all leave me alone with June please." She would never know it, but those words cut me deep. Not wanting to let the nigga make it, I decided to be petty.

"Come on son, let this man talk to mommy. We will come back later." Now the nigga's face looked just like mine. As soon as we got in the hallway, I needed Akina to do me a favor.

"Can you take Ty to your house. I'll come back and get him. I don't want him around that nigga, and I need to talk to my brother alone?" Nodding, she got the keys from Meek, and left with Ty. Motioning for him to walk with me, I explained to him what the fuck was going on.

"This nigga showed up at my house. That's why Malae passed out. This nigga trying to take my family, and I'm thinking I'm gone have to break my promise. He not just about to take my bitch, but I don't know his motives for coming back. I can't let this nigga come for my family bro." The look on his face let me know I wasn't about to like what he was gone say.

"Bro I know you love her, and you're scared to lose a family again. This is something you gone have to let her decide on her own. If you take her decision from her, she will never forgive you. Trust in love bro. Yall

have something special, believe in that."

"Okay, but if she chooses him, I'm not letting they

ass make it. Yall got me fucked up. Can you do me a

favor though just in case she chooses me?"

"Anything bro." Telling him what I wanted done, I

gave him my keys and he left. Heading back to the room,

I figured they talked enough. I ain't about to give his ass

no leeway.

MEEK...

It seems like me and my brother always go

through shit, at the same damn time. No matter what

though, I always had to put my shit to the side, and

make sure my baby bro was okay. He was like my son,

and I had to protect him at all costs. If June was back

from the dead on some bullshit, I was gone kill him

myself.

My brother came to far to let some thieving ass

clown, come push him back to those depressed ass days.

Malae had changed him, but I could see the look in his

eye. He wanted to kill June so bad, and I hope he

listened to me. She won't choose him as default, she will

resent him.

The hurt was killing him, but he was putting on a

good front. Heading to the jewelry store, I picked out a

ring for him. If she chose him, he never wanted

someone else to be able to come in and threaten what

they had. That type of love had me calming down

towards Akina. The shit hurt a nigga to his soul, but I know that wasn't her intent. We been together long enough for me to know she didn't mean to hurt me. The fact that she was scared, and couldn't trust that I had her back, means I failed as her nigga. If my girl was insecure, that shit was on me. If she too scared to tell me something is hurting her, I failed as a protector.

A nigga ain't never failed at shit in life, and I wasn't about to start now. It was up to me to fix us, and I needed to make sure she knew and understood that I had her in every aspect of life. She was a reflection of me, and don't know what fear is. Grabbing what I needed, I headed to the house, so we could talk.

When I got in the door, her and Ty were playing the game, and it looked like she was winning. It would be fucked up if that nigga June was able to come back and take him away. We all loved this nigga like he came out Modest's nut sack. This was our lil nigga, and I couldn't even imagine him not being around.

"Ty, do Uncle Meek a favor. Go upstairs and play in your room, and I'll be up there to kick your ass in a minute. You got me?"

"Yes. Don't forget. Last time you forgot and left me playing by myself." This lil nigga was something else.

"I got you." Last time I was in his Auntie guts, and I forgot. When he was out of ear shot, I pulled Akina to me.

"What you get me for Valentine's Day?" She looked confused.

"Nothing baby, it was supposed to be for Gabbie, and then with what happened earlier, I didn't think you wanted to still be here."

"Can I request a gift?" She nodded her head. "Can you please give me the chance to be a father. I understand why you were scared, and if I had done my job as your man, you wouldn't have been. Just let me show you that I got you."

"I will give you a million babies as long as you don't leave me. I love you so much, and I promise, I won't ever make a decision without you again."

"Good, now I don't have to beat your ass. Now give me some pussy, but it gotta be quick. I have to whoop his ass in this game, and take him back to the hospital." Dancing in front of me, she slowly started to take off her clothes. It was gone be hard, but I was gone

try my best to hit these guts quick.

MALAE...

June showing up had me in my fucking feelings.

After giving birth, I realized that I wanted and needed

my family. I could see the hurt and nervousness in

Modest's eyes, but he had my heart now. I know that

me and June have history, but that part of my life was

over.

Not to mention, his ass ain't shit. It's been almost

two years, and he just now showing his face. He let me,

and his son grieve him, knowing he wasn't dead. What

kind of nigga would do that to the person that he

supposedly loves? Hell, what kind of nigga would do that

to his kid.

When he walked in the room, I knew I needed to

tell his ass this wasn't that. I wouldn't allow anyone to

come in and fuck up my family. Me and Modest had

come a long way, and the fact that Ty didn't even

acknowledge him said a lot.

The look on Modest's face when I asked to speak

to June broke my heart. I wasn't trying to be with this

nigga, the only thing I worried about was Modest going

back to his old ways and trying to kill June again. I didn't

want that. It scared me to see the look in his eyes, and I

refused to let him go back to being that guy.

"June look, I know that we have a lot of history

together. A child, and a lot of love. When you left, our

world shattered, but Modest helped us pick up the

pieces. He is my everything now, and I'm not about to

leave him. We can work out visitation for your son, but

other than that, we are done."

"You gone stay with the nigga that tried to kill me.

You're dumber than I thought, and I should have been

left your ass. That nigga got me walking around in a

damn shit bag, and you can sit in my face saying you not

leaving him. Fuck you, and fuck YOUR son. You can keep

the mother fucker." When he turned to walk away,

Modest knocked his ass out.

"Nigga talking shit walking around smelling like

death and booty. You better had chosen me, or your ass

was gone be walking around smelling like shitty shitty

bang bang." Holding his finger up while I laughed, he

dragged his ass into the hallway. "Let the nurses deal with his outside booty ass. That nigga wasn't getting my son anyway. I would have beat your ass if you sent him with that nigga. You see his ass in them Sketchers, not my son."

"I love your mean ass, and you better not kill him Modest. We're good, and you don't have to worry, I'm not going anywhere. You're stuck with my ass." Kissing me, he moaned against my lips.

"This gone be a long six weeks. Give me my baby. I need to turn her against your ass too." Meek, Ty, and Akina walked back in.

"Speaking of love, Malae, I love your ass more than you could ever know. You got me so gone, I'll kill your pussy to save your ass." We all looked around the room trying to figure out what the fuck his ass was

talking about. "Yall know what the fuck I'm saying.

Bottom line, you're my family. You and Ty have given me

so much, and I never want you to feel like I ain't got you.

You gave my baby my last name, and now I want to give

you my last name. Will you marry me?"

Ty screamed louder than I did. This man was my

world, and I loved the shit out of this man.

"Yes baby. Yes."

"I was gone wait until Valentine's Day, but we are

doing it for Gabbie with bro and them. Just know that I

always got you." He kissed me again, as I cried tears of

joy.

AKINA...

It was so much love in the air, you couldn't do shit but appreciate Valentine's Day. We all got dressed in Gabbie's favorite color pink. The guys even wore pink button downs. Meek went all out and we rode in a stretch limousine. Bought a million balloons, a cake, and roses for her grave.

Walking up, today was emotional. I haven't cried over her in a while, but Meek made it so special, the shit got to me. Feeling him wiping my tears, I found strength to keep going. Kneeling, I placed my rose on her headstone.

"I love you so much baby girl. Happy Valentine's Day. Mommy misses you every day. You're about to have a brother or a sister, and I need you to look after them. Keep watching over mommy, and I promise I will never forget you." Meek kneeled and laid his rose down.

"You have the most amazing mommy in the world. You brought us together, and I promise to take care of her. You have given her the greatest love she has ever known, and it's only right we give it back to you. If it's alright with you, I would like to pick up where you left off. Akina, can I give you all the love I know you deserve? Can I be your all? Can I be your husband?" When he pulled out a ring, I damn near passed out.

"Yes. Thank you so much for everything." Modest, Malae, and Ty laid their roses down and said a few words. After everyone was done, we released the heart shaped balloons in my daughter's honor. I will never forget this day, and if I didn't know before, I knew on

today this man stole my heart.

MY GUTTA

VALENTINE

☐

REASON NUMBER FOURTEEN

"Tell me how long you been this way. Maybe I can open up your heart. See I've been waiting all my life for someone just like you, and I know you've been waiting too. For someone to love you. All you need is someone who cares. Someone who will always be there."

Someone To Love You- Ruff Endz

PROLOGUE...

NAE...

Standing in the mirror, I gave myself a once over. Tonight had to be perfect, and I needed everything to go as planned. Me and Gutta been dating for a month now and it was time shit changed. As fine as I was, I never encountered a guy that didn't try to have sex with me. A bitch never even been to his house. he took me on a bunch of dates, and spoiled my ass rotten, but that was as far as anything went.

Making sure my dress hugged me in all the right places, and my ass was popping. I went to answer the door when I heard the bell. This nigga stood there looking at me and I was ready to say fuck everything. He leaned against the door in his button down, but his tattoos still found a way to show. When the nigga licked his lips, my pussy jumped.

"You ready to go beautiful?" Clearing my throat, I finally found my voice.

"Yes." Heading out, we slid in his black on black Spider Maserati. He held my hand, and his touch had my ass on fire. When we pulled up to his massive ass mansion, I was confused.

"Where are we?" Looking over at me, he smiled with his perfect white teeth.

"My place." Shit that wasn't hard at all. Here I was thinking of ways not to fail tonight, and making sure I had his ass balls deep in this pussy. Climbing out the car, he came to my side and let me out. A bitch was nervous as hell, as he punched in the codes.

As soon as we stepped in, the smell of seafood hit my nose. It smelled so good, too bad that shit was going to waste.

"Where is your bathroom?" He pointed down the hall, and I mustered up the sexiest walk I could.

GUTTA...

Being the King of Houston, I had a lot of mother fuckers after me, and that made a nigga smarter. Bitches threw the pussy at me left and right, but over the years I learned not to think with my dick head. It wasn't a bitch in Houston that didn't want to be Gutta's wife, but I screened these hoes like they were applying for a bank job.

Before I even stick my dick in a bitch, they went through an extensive background check, and they ass didn't even know it. Some bitches moved on, and told the

next hoe I was gay, and some after finding out who they

were, I wouldn't let them lick my balls. A nigga like me

wasn't pressed for pussy, money made me cum. What I

needed was a down ass bitch willing to ride with me. She

needed to be able to handle my lifestyle, and not nag a

nigga every damn day.

Watching Nae walk away, my dick jumped. This

was one fine ass chick, and it was hard for me not to fuck

her while she was being screened. When she walked

back out, her ass straddled me and slid her tongue in my

mouth.

"Fuck dinner, let's go upstairs." Grabbing her by

her ass, I carried her to my bedroom never breaking our

kiss. Snatching her dress off, I had to control myself looking at her body.

"Damn." She smirked as I removed my clothes. She took control, and laid me on my back. Before I could stop her, she slid down on my dick. Her pussy was so tight and wet, I almost forgot she was on my shit without a condom. It was like she knew I was about to lift her up, cus her ass started going ham on my shit. I wasn't about to let her fuck the shit out of me, so I spread her ass and took charge. No bitch on this earth was gone say they fucked the shit out of Gutta.

She leaned down on me and sat back up. When I heard the gun cock back, I laughed.

"Is something funny?" She pointed the gun right between my eyes, and I grabbed her and kept right on *fucking the bitch. She was battling with herself on what she was supposed to do, or if she wanted to enjoy these ten inches I was dropping in her.*

"Fuck." Her body started shaking, and I smiled. Knowing it didn't matter, I let my nut off in her.

"So you just gone nut in my bitch?" When I heard Franco's voice, I laughed again.

"Fuck yeah. Her pussy was tight as African braids." She climbed off, and he walked all the way in my room. Him and four other niggas had guns drawn on me.

"You think this shit a game? Nigga you about to lose." Franco was one of my biggest enemies, and the nigga been after me for years. His old ass needed to let it go. I stood up, and put my briefs back on. They all looked at me like I was crazy.

"Nigga you walking around this mother fucker like you ain't about to die." Smirking again, I walked over to Nae and kissed her.

"Such a fucking waste." Franco started towards me, when he heard all the guns cock back. Turning around, the room was filled with my niggas. Like I said, I screened every bitch, and this hoe had me fucked up. Reaching in my drawer, I grabbed my gun. It's about to get ugly in this mother fucker.

?

CHAPTER ONE GUTTA...

Standing on the block with my niggas, it was nothing like summer time in Houston. The bitches be out, and the block be sewed up like a night club. We were all sitting around shooting the shit, when a group

of bitches walked up choosing. This yellow bitch walked

up, and you could tell she thought she was the shit.

"Hey Gutta. You ready to stop playing and give me

some of that dick?" Running her hands down my chest, I

was already annoyed.

"Hey Chi, don't you hate when a bitch thinks just

because she light skinned, she fine? Hoe over here

looking like dressed up Shephard's Pie. Get your ugly ass

on. It's too hot bruh." She was pissed, but me and Chi

continued to talk shit.

"She got a light skinned friend looking like Michael

Jackson." Laughing at Chi, I joined in singing the song.

Walking off, she tried her best to make a dramatic exit,

but she couldn't.

"Hey girl, your heels just won't let you make it. them bitches leaning. We gone call them mother fuckers Scape goats." Everybody started laughing. Her friends didn't want to leave, but the look we gave let them know they wasn't getting no play.

"This scene dead than a mother fucker. Let's go hit up Treasures." Chi ass always wanted to go hang out at the strip club, but it was so dry outside, I didn't mind tonight. My business and money were running smoothly, so I had time. Walking over to our cars, a group of bitches pulled up in front of the store. Now this chick caught my attention like a mother fucker. She was about five five, pretty chocolate skin, and she was rocking her real hair. She was petite, but her booty was looking perfect in her shorts. Wearing some Calamine retro J's, I knew she was my kind of girl. Dipping back, I stepped to her.

"Hey shorty what's good? I'm Gutta."

"Brinx, and I'm not interested." She shot me down quick as hell. That let me know she wasn't from around here. All the chicks in my city knew who I was, and wanted me. It made me want her more. She wasn't ran through from the hood niggas, and she wasn't after my status.

"Trust me, you will change your mind. I'm that nigga." Trying not to sound salty, I wanted her to know I still wanted her, but don't play me left.

"You that bright ass nigga. Damn turn off." Her and the girls she was with laughed at my expense. Not about to let her ass front me in my shit, I clapped back.

"Don't get mad at me because your ass a field nigga. Clown ass. Grab some carmex while you in there too with your chapped lip ass. Issa herpe." Walking off, I left her there trying to check out her lips. Climbing in my whip, Chi tried to go in.

"That bitch tried to go. I knew you was about to let her ass have it." Giving him my serious face, I cut him off.

"Don't call my girl no bitch. Tell Jeff to run a background check on her. Ms field nigga just met her match. Now let's go watch these hoes shake dat ass."

MAKE SURE YOU CHECK OUT THAT GUTTA LOVE COMING IN MARCH.....

KEEP UP WITH LATOYA NICOLE

Like my author page on fb @misslatoyanicole

My fb page Latoya Nicole Williams

IG Latoyanicole35

Twitter Latoyanicole35

Snap Chat iamTOYS

Reading group: Toy's House of Books

?

OTHER BOOKS BY LATOYA NICOLE

NO WAY OUT: MEMOIRS OF A HUSTLA'S GIRL

NO WAY OUT 2: RETURN OF A SAVAGE

GANGSTA'S PARADISE

GANGSTA'S PARADISE 2: HOW DEEP IS YOUR LOVE

ADDICTED TO HIS PAIN (STANDALONE)

LOVE AND WAR: A HOOVER GANG AFFAIR

LOVE AND WAR 2: A HOOVER GANG AFFAIR

LOVE AND WAR 3: A HOOVER GANG AFFAIR

LOVE AND WAR 4: A GANGSTA'S LAST RIDE

CREEPING WITH THE ENEMY: A SAVAGE STOLE MY

HEART 1-2

I GOTTA BE THE ONE YOU LOVE (STANDALONE)

THE RISE AND FALL OF A CRIME GOD: PHANTOM AND

ZARIA'S STORY

THE RISE AND FALL OF A CRIME GOD 2: PHANTOM AND

ZARIA'S STORY

ON THE 12TH DAY OF CHRISTMAS MY SAVAGE GAVE TO

ME

A CRAZY KIND OF LOVE: PHANTOM AND ZARIA

?

BOOK 17, AND I CAN'T BELIEVE IT. FOUR NUMBER ONES, I'M STILL IN DISBELIEF. YOU GUYS ARE AWESOME, AND I LOVE YOU. THANK YOU FOR CONTINOUSLY MAKING MY BOOKS A SUCCESS. WITHOUT YOU THERE IS NO ME. MAKE SURE YOU DOWNLOAD, SHARE, READ AND REVIEW. MORE BOOKS WILL BE COMING FROM ME. BE ON THE LOOK OUT. MLPP WE BRINGING THE HEAT.

THE HOOVER GANG WILL BE BACK IN SHADOW OF A GANGSTA AND MAKE SURE YOU LOOK OUT FOR THAT GUTTA LOVE COMING IN MARCH.

CPSIA information can be obtained
at www.ICGtesting.com
Printed in the USA
LVOW13s1136050618
579618LV00016B/231/P